Kezia and Rosie

Rebecca Burns

First published 2022 by Dahlia Publishing Ltd
ISBN 9781913624095

Copyright © Rebecca Burns 2022

The moral right of the author has been asserted.

All rights reserved. No part of this publication may be reproduced, stored in or introduced into a retrieval system, or transmitted, in any form, or by any means (electronic, mechanical, photocopying, recording or otherwise) without the prior written permission of the publisher. Any person who does any unauthorized act in relation to this publication may be liable to criminal prosecution and civil claims for damages.

Printed and bound by Grosvenor Group

One of the stories in this collection has appeared elsewhere, in a slightly different form:

'The Allotment Gate' in *Blake Jones Review*.

This book is sold subject to the condition that it shall not, by way of trade or otherwise, be lent, re-sold, hired out, or otherwise circulated without the publisher's prior consent in any form of binding or cover other than that in which it is published and without a similar condition including this condition being imposed on the subsequent purchaser.

This is a work of fiction. Unless otherwise indicated, all the names, characters, businesses, places, events and incidents in this book are either the product of the author's imagination or used in a fictitious manner. Any resemblance to actual persons, living or dead, or actual events is purely coincidental.

A CIP catalogue record for this book is available from The British Library.

For Gladys and Frank. Two people who were the epitome of love.

And for my little sister, Claire.

Contents

The Allotment Gate	1
The Gypsy Caravan	9
The Chip Shop	18
The Jewellery Box	27
The Storm	39
The Phone Call	48
The Bread Poultice	60
The Ferrets	71
The Birthday	82
The Library	94
The Visit	108

Acknowledgements
About the Author

The Allotment Gate

The first rung is the worst. It shouldn't be, it doesn't make sense, not when Kezia considers it, as it's on the bottom, closest to the pavement, so if you fall you won't exactly hurt yourself or break your ankle. Not like that time she jumped from the top of the stairs to the bottom, just to see if she could, and then Dad was mad at her as he had to miss Grandstand to take her to casualty.

No, if you fall off the bottom rung you won't break anything, but that's not why it's the worst. It's because every time Grandad swings the gate and you're standing on the wooden slat, the gate does something like slap up against the pole, and then shake, so every bone feels like it's shivering inside you. Kezia doesn't know the word for it, to describe what it feels like, just like she doesn't know the word for the thin skin on the side of her head that makes shapes bloom in her eyes when she presses down hard, and the word for the thick silence that lies in the house when both her parents are in the same room – it's black and heavy and lies like a rug, like Grandma's old dog who snores and farts in front of Sherlock Holmes after tea. Only, she likes to cuddle Missy, when she isn't too smelly, and when the silence between Mum and Dad creeps into the house she doesn't want to cuddle it. She wants to run away.

But you have to stand on the first rung. It's part of the game. Even Rosie knows it, and she's only five. You stand on the first rung and then Grandad swings the gate. Then you move up to the next one.

It's a good day when Grandad swings the gate for the whole game. Almost as good as the days Grandma gives them twenty-five pence to buy a pat of ice-cream from Mr George Whippy Esquire in his pink and blue van with the huge plastic cone on the roof. A day when Grandad does all the swings and they get an ice-cream is beyond special. Kezia can remember only one day like that recently and that was at the start of the summer holidays, when they'd first come to stay.

Today Grandad has done the first swing for Rosie – it always has to be Rosie who goes first as she is the youngest. This has never felt fair to Kezia but *okay* – but then Grandad leaves them to fetch salad from his allotment patch. It isn't far, they can see him, and that's the rule Grandma set. He can potter around the allotment all he wants and leave the girls on the gate, as long as they can see each other. Grandma's read a lot of stories in newspapers with red tops, and they make her suck her teeth and grab the girls in fierce hugs that smell of tea and rosewater.

They can see Grandad now, bald head bending over his lettuces and radishes. He's red around the ears. Maybe it's sunburn.

'Come on, Kezia!' Rosie is getting cross. Her little mouth is pressed up into a line. She looks like their mum when she's picking up clothes off the floor or getting the hoover out.

'Calm the frig down,' Kezia mutters, knowing she's said a word she shouldn't have, but it is too tempting not to try it out. She'd sneaked downstairs one night and watched the telly while Grandma and Grandad snored and Rosie took over the whole single bed. Someone on a programme about popstars from Europe had said it and the person asking the questions – interviewer? Was that the word? – had laughed. *Frigging awesome, man, was such a trip.*

Rosie makes her eyes round. 'I'm telling on you!'

'Then I won't push you on the gate.'

A stand-off. They both have power. This summer has changed things and how their world works.

The second rung. This is better. Air slaps around Rosie's legs as Kezia swings her, the girl's shoes from Clarks squeaking and twisting as she keeps her balance. Sometimes Kezia thinks she likes the second rung the best, because it still isn't too far from the ground and yet is high enough to feel like a ride, belly swooping like she's in one of those dodgem cars at the Wakes in town. She can't be certain, though, that it is her favourite. She used to be so sure of everything – which member of Bananarama she liked best, which vegetable she would eat first so it was gone, gone – but now the world feels like a trembling, spinning plate.

Rosie's dress flutters as the gate swings and slaps, and for a second Kezia is afraid that the blue fabric with tiny yellow daisies will catch on a nail or a splinter of wood and tear. It has happened before and there were sobs on the way back to Grandma's. Grandma fixed it. Of course she did, she'd made Mum's wedding dress. They'd always known that, though Mum doesn't mention it as much these days. But dresses cost money – Kezia doesn't really understand what that means, only that broken things make their Dad cross. Grandma managed to sew Rosie's dress back together so well Mum didn't even notice. Only Rosie and Kezia knew, the seam linking the ripped pieces of fabric back together like a pale scar.

The dress doesn't tear. Rosie is laughing. The second rung is her favourite and she's certain about that.

Over her shoulder, in the field, Grandad is shouting at something in the grass, probably a rabbit. Sometimes a rabbit ends up in Grandma's pot. Kezia's held one before, a dead one, still warm. Rosie shrieked and ran away when Grandad held it up, snare still round its neck, but Kezia didn't mind. Its fur was so soft her fingertips barely felt it. When she tucked it inside her cardigan so no one would see on the walk home, it flattened against her chest, a warm loaf. She asked Grandad if she could keep it in her bed and he'd laughed and said it would soon become stiff and stink. Besides, rabbits made good eating.

Today's rabbit has avoided the snare and appears to have eaten some of Grandad's radishes. Kezia watches as he picks up a rake and starts swinging it at the creature, back and forth, and he's shouting again. Kezia's mouth falls open. The gate glides to a halt and Rosie watches as well, both girls silent. Grandad, who lets them trace the faded navy tattoos on his arm or comb his hair with their doll's make-up set, is spitting out words that they just know are bad. Kezia hasn't heard them on the late-night telly, but the shortness of them, the way the words hang like barks and seem to stab the air – they are of the adult world, the world of black fogs held within walls, of hissed conversations Mum and Dad have when they think the girls are asleep.

The gate stills completely and the rake swings and their Grandad rages.

The third rung is the last one you can stand on. Rosie steps onto it. When Kezia turns to look at her little sister it is as though she is seeing her in a dream. Rosie's body is bent forward so she can balance and grip the top of the gate. She's being brave. At the start of the summer holidays she couldn't do it, daren't do it. Not even Grandad's encouragement could entice her onto the rung. But she's been doing it for the last two weeks, since the last day their Mum rang to speak to them. Rosie steps onto the third rung now with a smug, proud look on her little face.

Kezia pushes her slowly. Grandad is still yelling at the rabbit and Kezia thinks she might get a slap if she scares Rosie by swinging the gate too hard. Grandad's only slapped her legs once, when she tried to run across the road to Mr George Whippy Esquire's van and a neighbour nearly squashed her in his Robin Reliant. Then he'd cried because he felt bad, which was somehow worse than the sting on Kezia's bare legs. She doesn't want to see him cry today. Not any day.

So she pushes her sister gently and Rosie settles and sighs

on the third rung. Kezia swings her for a long time and they watch Grandad out on his allotment. He's thrown the rake down now and is stomping around, slamming his feet down heavily on the earth. Rosie giggles softly. Kezia sees Grandad's tight fists and the way he blinks rapidly and doesn't laugh.

'Quiet, Rosie,' she murmurs. 'If you're quiet, I'll push you for longer.'

The fourth rung. This is the last rung and is one to sit on. No one would dream of standing on the fourth rung – it's right at the top of the gate! Kezia holds the gate still while Rosie throws a leg over and shakily sits down. Yesterday was the first time she managed to balance on the top without anyone holding her hand. She grins at Kezia when she's settled onto her perch.

'I did it again!'

'Well done, Rosie.' Kezia offers her a small smile but feels an ache in her chest like something has folded in her heart.

She remembers the first time she clambered to the top rung on her own. Rosie was in her buggy, pushed by Grandma. Mum held the allotment gate. In the field, where grass and Old Man's Beard grew up to the knee, Grandad showed Dad his rows of peas and corn, and Dad pretended to be interested. When he came back to the gate he kissed Kezia enthusiastically, and she squeaked she'd sat on the top rung all by herself.

'Such a big girl, Kez!' he'd cheered, and she'd caught the look he cast at Mum. She hated the shortening of Kezia's name. When Mum helped her down onto the path she squeezed Kezia's hand harder than needed.

Grandad is coming back. He holds a bundle of radishes and a lettuce. Kezia peeps at him, while holding out her arm for Rosie to grab and clamber down. She can't see a rabbit, and air she hasn't realised she is holding, escapes from her throat.

'Ready then, girls?' his voice is gruff. He is slightly out of breath, though the rake he'd been throwing is nowhere to be seen. 'Grandma will have tea ready.'

'Kezia hasn't had a swing,' Rosie protests, but Kezia shakes her head.

'It doesn't matter.' It really doesn't, the gate doesn't pull on her right now. In fact, she wants to be as far away from it as possible. The image of her Grandad wheeling a rake around his head and shouting at a brown bundle of fur seems to bleed into the motion of the allotment gate, slapping back and forth. She wants to be back in Grandma's kitchen, with Rosie, for suddenly that seems to be the only place that makes sense.

Grandad is frowning down at her. He looks like he's doing a crossword, one of those easy ones he sometimes does with his morning tea, before taking Kezia and Rosie into the garden so Grandma can clean. Then his brow clears. 'Let's go then, shall we? I reckon I can smell Grandma's baking. Maybe your Mum will call after tea.'

He hauls Rosie down from the gate and plants a kiss on the top of her head. Then he holds out his hand for Kezia and the three head down the dirt track back towards home.

The Gypsy Caravan

Grandad brings home the inner tube of a roll of packing paper. He comes back from the shops, blue and white plastic bag held in one hand, and edges past Rosie's doll's pram in the kitchen doorway, and Kezia sees the tube first, before anything. Grandma sees the plastic bag and they hear her suck on the few teeth she has left, for she loathes waste and knows he forgot to take a Happy Shopper bag from under the stairs and probably had paid 2p for the rubbish blue and white one. On an ordinary morning, Kezia would sympathise and maybe even lift her head from her colouring book to catch Grandma's eye – he's forgotten again, how *maddening* (a word she'd heard Grandma mutter when on the phone, when the girls were supposed to be asleep) – but the cardboard tube under Grandad's arm has left her momentarily dumbfounded.

The moment she sees it, to when she knows what to do with it, is separated by time the thickness of a butterfly's wing. Kezia's little face pinches and she stares at Grandad and the thing he carries so casually and she imagines what she'll make. She sees a riot of colours; blues and greens and yellows, and deep, deep burgundy, the colour of the wine Mum drank last year on holiday when Dad got enough overtime for a package deal to Malaga. Kezia didn't understand what a package deal meant, still doesn't, but it seemed to involve being allowed to take a suitcase, which was good because she didn't fancy wearing the same dress for two weeks. And Rosie still wet the bed, so they definitely had to take her rubber sheet and lots and lots of pants, so a suitcase was useful, really. Kezia blinks and Grandad is still there with the cardboard, and she can still see colours and knows *exactly* what she will do with that tube.

She will use it to make a gypsy caravan, like the one they saw on Blue Peter last week. She'll colour it in so carefully and neatly that *its beauty will leave her breathless*. Nelson said that to Emma Hamilton on the film last night and Kezia hasn't got over it. At bath time, while Grandma was brushing Rosie's hair in the room the sisters shared, Kezia said it in front of the mirror, and when she pressed her hand to her chest, she could feel her heart thrum beneath her nightie.

The only problem is, Rosie has seen the cardboard tube, too. She looks up as Grandad comes back in, having spent the morning rolling the inner of two slices of bread into tiny balls and dropping them in a mug of Bovril, which she has developed an endless taste for. Grandma doesn't mind at all and has even bought her a special mug, a post-box red one saying BOVRIL across it. It's Rosie's third mug of the morning. Kezia isn't convinced her sister really likes Bovril, only the claggy, gummy wet balls of dough she spoons out, but Rosie can get away with quite a bit these days, since last Christmas and her arm.

Rosie gasps and claps her hands, and flakes of moist bread splat on the kitchen table. Kezia is disgusted, and when Rosie starts lisping around the gap in her front teeth, wants to cram her little sister's face onto the wooden surface.

'Where'd you get that, Grandad?'

It is, Kezia accepts, a fair question. And a sinking realisation lines her stomach like a Sunday dinner. What if Grandad brought the cardboard tube home for him, for his use? He might want to post something somewhere – maybe to Uncle Andy in Australia – and *that* would be the end of *that*. No Gypsy Caravan for Kezia. Not even the fairy-tale of Uncle Andy in Australia could sweeten the disappointment.

'Did you get the haslet?' Grandma asks. It's Tuesday and they always have haslet sandwiches for dinner, with sliced tomatoes from the greenhouse, if there are any. Grandad's tomatoes taste better than any Kezia has ever had – better than the slimy, boring slices Mum used to put in her school lunchbox. It's summer when she eats Grandad's tomatoes.

'Bernard?' Grandma uses Grandad's full name. She's tired. She hasn't wanted to play Snakes and Ladders today.

'I did.' Grandad lays the plastic bag carefully on the table, as carefully as he buried the mangled carcass of a blackbird the cat brought in – another thing Kezia hasn't got over – and he sets his palm against the metal teapot. 'Still warm. Get me a mug, Rosie.'

The smell of the sliced meat wakes Missy, lying as usual beside the unlit gas fire. The dog lifts her nose hopefully and Kezia looks at her, at the deep velvet of her fur and the soft, flat paws that tap-tap-tap when she pads outside for a pee. Kezia feels a tang of love for Missy and decides to slip her some haslet from her sandwich.

'And my pills? Did the chemist have them?' Grandma asks.

'They did.'

Grandad pulls out a chair and sits down, and slips off his shoes. He's wearing grey socks and when he eases them from his feet, Kezia seems faint tramlines where the ribbing has clung his flesh tightly. 'Ah, that's better,' he says. He watches as Rosie pours him tea and pats her head.

This doesn't bode well for the cardboard tube and who will claim it. Kezia clears her throat. She keeps her eyes on her colouring book and tries to speak casually, oh so casually. 'What's the tube for, Grandad?'

Rosie shoots her a look. Again, not good. Rosie must also have plans. Inwardly Kezia scoffs. Her sister probably wants to build a raft for her Barbie, which she'll put in the bath and cry when the cardboard falls apart.

'Got it from Roy at the Post Office,' Grandad says. At the sink, Grandma stills and Kezia sees her elbows, like the skin of a turkey neck, rest on the steel frame. She doesn't turn round. That's weird, Kezia thinks. After a moment Grandma starts peeling potatoes again.

'Roy was throwing it away.' Grandad looks at Grandma's back and then quickly back to the girls. 'I thought you and Rosie might want it. You're always making things.'

It's unavoidable now. It will have to be shared between

them. Kezia tries to stay positive. It's a big tube. Enough to make a gypsy caravan, or even two, with her half. And if Rosie clogs up the plughole in the bath with her Barbie float, well, extra points.

'Yes, please, Grandad,' and she gives him her best smile, the one she had practised for the photographer at school. The teacher had made a funny noise when she'd bared her teeth and made her eyes like buttons, and she was sure she'd heard her whisper something to the photographer – *family situation, altered living arrangements* – but it was a good smile and Grandma had put the photograph of the sisters in the parlour.

'Here you go then.' Grandad places the tube on the table and Kezia and Rosie stare at it. Then they glance at each other. How to split it? Kezia knows better than to make a grab for it, for Rosie will shriek and squeeze out tears. Their fights have to be done away from the adults now, in the single bed at night or in the garden, when Grandma is making lunch.

'Will you cut it in half, Grandad?' Rosie asks. Her voice is like honey and extra nice. Kezia hates her a little and then thinks how like their Mum she sounds. She phones every three or four days now to speak to the girls. *Just a few more weeks, darling. You like it at Grandma and Grandad's anyway, don't you?*

Then Kezia doesn't want the tube. Her mouth feels very full, watery, like she used to feel in Dad's car when he had a Saturday free and took her to the football. It was a long drive into town. She was sick more than once, her thighs sticking to the leather on the back seat, puke dripping into the footwell. One time Dad was so angry with her he didn't speak to her for the whole first half and she was hoisted onto the shoulder of his mate instead, on the terrace. He hadn't minded the smell of vomit and gave her a hug, saying his own girl did the same.

'You have it, Rosie,' she says abruptly. 'Make something for your Barbie.'

Rosie narrows her eyes, distrustful. 'Don't you want it?'

'Course you do.' Grandad is watching them. He holds his mug to his lips and Kezia knows that it will only take moments for him to drink his tea. He'll open his mouth and pour it down, past his dentures, into his pale pink throat, and he'll smack his lips and wipe his mouth in the way he always does, and then he'll pour another and take his time over this one. Maybe he'll find a biscuit or two. He does just that, draining his mug. But he doesn't reach for the teapot again. Instead he rummages around in one of his huge trouser pockets, held up around his waist with brown string – belts an unnecessary affectation – and fishes out his penknife.

Kezia and Rosie eye it. The penknife. An item definitely not to touch or even think about touching. Grandma has few rules – eating with your mouth closed (which Rosie seems to bypass every meal) and they can't go to the allotment on their own – but not touching the penknife is the biggest. Grandad flexes the blade open slowly and runs a thick fingertip across the blade. 'Oh, yes,' he says. 'Could gut a Nazi bugger with that, all right.'

'Bernard.' Grandma at the sink.

But the girls know she isn't really cross. There are certain things Grandad will say, whether he is allowed to or not, and then grin and remind them he'd been a sailor in the war. It seems to give him a pass. Now he stands up and stretches his arms like a wrestler on the telly on a Saturday morning, about to deliver a killer blow, and makes swift work of cutting the cardboard tube in two. It isn't exactly an even split, but Grandad is not one for measuring – the rickety greenhouse is testament to that – but it's close enough. Rosie grabs the biggest piece. Kezia takes the smaller. Now she holds it in her hands, the gypsy caravan blooms again.

Then Grandad goes over to Grandma at the sink. He rests a hand on her shoulder and leans in, and for a moment Kezia thinks he's going to kiss her. Disgusting, she thinks. But he's speaking quietly. *Roy's going to phone his lad tonight.*

Kezia frowns. There is an overlay to the room, a layer of something unspoken that feels as heavy as a quilt. She knows it as surely as she knows Grandma mashes turnip through potato on Sundays, even though she never admits it. She hates knowing there's unspoken things in the air. It makes the world uncertain and wobbly, when it should be orderly or at least understandable. She thinks of the time she cut open her doll's head to see what was inside, what *exactly* made Belinda Bluebell blink so emphatically and sleep the second she was laid on her back, and how she made that tiny, cat-like noise when drinking from her plastic bottle of pretend milk. The ugliness of the wires in the doll's head made her scream and when Dad came running, he didn't understand at all. Instead he smacked her bottom for ruining her doll and threw poor old Belinda Bluebell in the bin.

Missy is snoring again and Rosie is humming at her elbow. Her sister hasn't noticed a thing. She's fetched Barbie from the bedroom and is measuring her against her half of the tube. But, something unexpected. She's brought a tube of nail varnish downstairs as well.

'What's that for?' Kezia asks. 'Is it mine?'

Rosie shakes her head quickly but looks away. 'It's mine. Grandad said it would make things waterproof.'

'How? It's nail varnish.'

Rosie shrugs. She's marked the tube so it's the same length as Barbie and Kezia knows she's going to ask Grandad to cut it to shape again.

'What are you making?' But Kezia thinks she knows and a feeling of disappointment creeps over her. Rosie isn't going to be sludging the bath plughole anytime soon.

'A raft for Barbie. And it'll float, Kez, it really will! I'm going to cover it in varnish.'

'You'll have to paint it outside. Nail varnish gives Grandma one of her heads.'

Grandma and Grandad are still whispering but Kezia can't hear anymore. She thinks they are still talking about Roy's son. She knows Roy and wonders if it was his son they'd met that one time when Grandad was posting a birthday present to Uncle Andy. He was dressed in a shiny grey suit and looked like a thinner, wonky version of Roy, as if he'd been bent through a circus mirror. He was the only person Kezia had ever seen, apart from on the telly, who carried a briefcase.

'Do you know who Roy's son is, Rosie?' she breathes. She edges closer to her sister, trying not to smell Bovril. The nail varnish surprises her. Maybe Rosie knows things.

But Rosie simply hums. She starts to draw on the cardboard tube, sketching out shaky, uneven oars and, checking that her grandparents aren't looking, starts to unscrew the bottle of varnish.

The Chip Shop

Saturday night and they are at the chip shop. Grandad has walked them down, holding both their hands, while Grandma stays behind and butters bread. She's promised if Kezia and Rosie are good and behave themselves while Grandad orders chips, she'll open the bottle of cherry pop as well. Rosie is almost faint with excitement and jerks her little legs down the street like a tin soldier.

Kezia is thrilled too but it's important not to show it. She's almost eight, and that's too old to be excited by chips. She nestles her hand in Grandad's and concentrates on the roughness of his skin like the bark of a tree. His hands are always warm. It's like being held by a sheet of sandpaper that's been left on the radiator. Sometimes he gives her a little squeeze, not painful but almost, to let her know he's there and loves her. It makes her feel as comfortable as a boiled egg.

'I'm going to have a fritter, aren't I Grandad?' Rosie is bouncing now. She's got a scrape on her elbow from chasing the neighbour's cat in the garden and Grandma smeared it with Savlon. Kezia gets a whiff every now and then. She can't decide if she likes it. It's a smell that seems to make the inside of her nose flare. It's not like the bar of Zest soap in the bathroom which she knows she definitely likes, though that also makes her eyes water in the mornings, and it's not like the smell of tea, tea, tea, which Grandma mashes in the silver pot every hour

'Yes, Rosie, you can have a fritter.' Grandad's voice sounds different this evening, as if he's far away. Kezia glances up at him, the frizz of hair around his ears framing his skull like candyfloss. There had been another phone call just before they left and Grandma had turned up the telly, making Tarzan yodel even harder, and Kezia couldn't hear what Grandad was muttering into the mouthpiece in the hallway. He's been different since he came off the call.

An awful thought strikes Kezia as they turn the street corner and see the chip shop in the distance. Maybe it was Mrs Hartley on the phone. Kezia's tummy curls up like the neighbour's cat does on the top of Grandad's greenhouse. Yesterday when Grandma walked them to the shops, Mrs Hartley was in her garden. Kezia's hand becomes clammy in Grandad's embrace, remembering. She'd stood beside Mrs Hartley's wall while Grandma and the whiskered old neighbour talked and, carefully, delicately, had pulled all the petals from a rose hanging over the pavement.

Kezia doesn't know why she did it. She remembers feeling angry, waking with a headache after Rosie had taken over the whole bed again, and she'd said something in a hard way to Grandma that earned her a glare. She'd pushed Rosie too high on the swing Grandad built in the garden, knowing her sister would shriek and maybe do a little wee, but not even that made her feel better. Her tummy hurt and hurt. It pinches again as she thinks of the roses, flowers so beautiful all she'd wanted to do up until yesterday is to pick one and bury her nose into its folded centre. Certainly not tear it into pieces. No one saw her do it – not Rosie, not Grandma, and definitely not Mrs Hartley who had a magnificent mole on her top lip that looked like a chocolate Revel. Kezia had crushed the petals under her sandal, rolling them back and forth into bleeding pink worms. For some reason, destroying the rose in such a way had made her feel better.

She wriggles her hand free of Grandad's grip and wipes it on her sun dress. Maybe Mrs Hartley counts her roses and the missing flower is like a child to her. Maybe it hurts her for a child to have disappeared, with only a snapped stalk as a sign it was once there.

'What do you think you'll have, Kezia?' Grandad's hand brushes the top of her head. 'Pea mix? Grandma's made mint sauce for the lamb tomorrow. Oh, mint sauce on top of mushy peas is lovely.'

Again his voice sounds weird, strained like the sounds Rosie makes when playing her recorder. Grandma sends her with Grandad to the allotment when she wants to practice, saying it sets her dentures on edge, which Kezia doesn't understand – how can teeth be on *edge*? On the edge of what? They are in your *mouth*.

'I hate mushy peas!' Rosie says happily. She's jumping from paving slab to paving slab, trying not to step on the cracks and break her mother's back. She hums. On Thursday Grandma let them stay up to watch Top of the Pops and Bananarama were on. 'Oh, what do those ladies sing about Venus being on fire?'

'Shut up,' Kezia says and earns a frown from Grandad but she doesn't care. Bananarama is *her* band. Her stomach ripples again. She'd better not have mushy peas. She'd fart in bed and Rosie would blab to Grandma.

'Here we are,' Grandad says. They are at the chip shop. They are early enough to miss the tea-time queue and there's only a couple of other people there. An old man, like Grandad, and another little girl. 'Ey up, Dave,' Grandad says to the bloke, and points to the corner of the shop, where the wooden forks and bottles of vinegar rest on a table. Kezia and Rosie go and stand beside it.

The chip shop is hot. Steam clouds the windows and Rosie starts to draw. She rubs a finger, still grubby from the garden, over the glass and creates a ragged butterfly. Then another, wonky shape, with four sticky legs. She nudges Kezia. 'That's Missy. You have a go.'

Kezia shakes her head. She doesn't like the feel of cold wet slime on her fingers. At school when all the others use their hands to make pictures and splat them in the paint she hangs back. Instead, she looks at the little girl and the man, now talking to Grandad. Grandad is smiling and nodding, but something about the way he stands makes Kezia feels nervous. He's pulled the shirt from his waistband, hiding the rope holding up his trousers, and one hand is on his hip. Grandad never stands like that.

'I'm Lucy who are you I'm six.' The girl has come over. She is wearing a blue dress with a white collar that Kezia recognises from the window of BHS in town. She stares at it. Tiny blue ladybirds are stitched on the edge of the collar and on the hem. *Blue ladybirds.* Kezia sighs with the magic of it all.

Rosie has turned from the window and, instinctively, sticks her fingers in her mouth. Kezia feels faintly sick.

'That's my grandad he's called Dave he's buying me fish and chips what are you having?'

Rosie stares. She edges closer to Kezia and her gaze falls to the girl's dress. She gasps. Kezia knows she's seen the blue ladybirds.

'I'm Rosie,' she says. She is terribly impressed.

Lucy narrows her eyes at Kezia. Her shoes are also blue and, glancing down, Kezia spots the impossible – there are blue ladybirds around the trim.

'Have you had sushi I had it last night.'

'What's sushi?' Rosie asks. Over her shoulder Grandad gives a strange laugh and nods his head rapidly. He's placed his order and leans against the counter, talking to Dave.

'It's raw fish I didn't like it but Grandma says it's important to try new things we went to a restaurant and it wasn't even my birthday.'

'You talk really fast,' Rosie says.

'Lucy?' Dave calls from the counter. 'Are you being nice?'

'Of course!' and Lucy throws the words in a way that makes Kezia's eyebrows shoot up into her hair. Dave walks over. He holds a package of chips under his arm, wrapped in newspaper, and smiles with all of his teeth at the girls. He's shorter than Grandad. His neck is thick and wedged and makes Kezia think of the fat on the top of an uncooked pork joint.

'Nice to see you both, Kezia and Rosie,' he says. Kezia blinks and wonders how he knows their names.

Grandad comes to stand beside them. His face is pink and there's something fixed and awkward about his mouth.

'That's a pretty dress, Lucy,' he says.

'Mummy bought it for me at the weekend look when I spin.' The girl gives a twirl and they see white lace underneath the blue fabric. Rosie pulls her head back into her shoulders. Kezia spots more blue ladybirds lining the lace. Her own dress, green, with the panel at the bottom that doesn't match - sewn in by Grandma to lengthen it - feels itchy against her skin.

'How's the arm now, Rosie?' Dave has a booming voice. He pats Rosie on the head. She squeaks and scuttles to stand next to Grandad. Dave laughs. 'Looks like it's healed ok. I know your Grandad was a bit worried about it.'

Kezia bites her lip. No one ever mentions Rosie's arm and what happened at Christmas. Grandad's mouth is working oddly, lips pulled in and out. He's started to sweat.

Rosie blinks rapidly. She looks like she's going to cry.

'Did you break it my brother broke his arm on our ski trip last year,' Lucy says proudly. She pokes Rosie's arm. 'Did you have pins I can see a little scar.'

Then Rosie does cry and buries her face in Grandad's shirt. Kezia clenches her fist. What a horrible girl. She wants to slap her.

Dave clears his throat. 'I'm sorry. Best to forget about it, eh? Never could keep my mouth shut. Your Grandad can tell you tales about me from work, can't you, Bernard!' He nudges Lucy. 'She takes after me, I'm afraid.'

Even Rosie, sobbing, knows it's time for Dave and his granddaughter to go now and stop talking. The group stand in an awkward circle. Only Lucy seems oblivious, staring at the scars just above Rosie's elbow as if she wants to touch them again.

'Right, best get home before these go cold,' and Dave nods emphatically. He touches Lucy's shoulder. 'Come on, treacle, say goodbye to Kezia and Rosie.'

'Goodbye Kezia and Rosie,' Lucy chants. She has a perfect button nose. She leans in and, astonishingly, kisses Kezia on both cheeks. Her hair smells of coconut.

Kezia rubs her face and glares at her. She thinks of Mrs Hartley's rose petals, scrubbed underfoot, and imagines Lucy's proud face under the sole of her shoe.

Dave laughs. 'Ignore that,' he says to Grandad. 'She picked it up in Austria last year, on that ski trip. Keeps doing it, even to the dog.'

'Grandma's got a dog. Missy,' Rosie says, shyly. Lucy's so strange she's made Rosie recover.

Dave nodded knowingly. 'Must be knocking on a bit now, that old girl. Lovely. How old?'

'Fifteen,' Grandad says faintly. 'We bought her for Anna but she stayed with us when she married.'

Kezia glances at him. Another transgression on this

eventful trip to the chip shop. Grandad doesn't say their mother's name. It's usually 'your mum' or 'your mother.' Her stomach hurts terribly.

'Right, well, we'll be off.' Dave switches the bag of chips from under one arm to another. 'Just one last thing, Bernard, before I forget – Roy said about you contacting his son?'

'Yes.' Grandad is barely audible.

'Well, I don't want to muddy the water, but if you're going in a certain direction, Lucy's father is a solicitor too. Successful, you know. I'm sure I could have a word with him.'

Grandad sways a little. His temples are wet and what's left of his hair sticks to it in messy clumps. He doesn't reply but instead gives the tiniest movement of his head.

'We'll be off then.' And with that, Dave catches his granddaughter's hand and heads for the door. Just as he does, the man behind the counter shouts that their fritters are ready and Grandad shakes his head, as if throwing off dizziness. He wanders over with Rosie to collect them.

Kezia watches Dave and Lucy plod down the street towards a shiny car and get in. They drive by as Grandad is paying and Lucy waves. Kezia pretends not to see.

When Grandad returns with the chips, he's blinking. He clears his throat. Kezia thinks he's about to speak, to explain and say something about Roy's son, and doesn't want him to. She doesn't want him to say anything

'I wish I'd had mushy peas last night!' she blurts out.

'Why?' Rosie pulls a face.

'So I could stand right next to Lucy and fart and turn those stupid blue ladybirds green.'

At that, Grandad laughs. It's a proper, big laugh, right from his belly. The man behind the counter looks up, wondering what's going on, but Grandad roars and roars. He's still chuckling as they leave the shop and walk down the street towards home, and still going when he puts the chips on the kitchen table next to Grandma's buttered bread.

The Jewellery Box

Grandma is letting the girls look in her jewellery box. It is such a special treat that Rosie can barely contain herself and makes small whimpering sounds as she stands beside the dresser. A shiver ripples through her body. Kezia feels it, and it is like a wave, lulling her into her sister's joy, threatening to overwhelm her own hard little body and steeled heart. There is a smell to Rosie, too, hot and soapy. Kezia inhales it; it makes her nose sweat. She thinks of the shoreline at Ilfracombe, where they went on holiday before Rosie was born, and the brace of briny, whipped water. She clears her throat, fighting not to be overwhelmed. She reminds herself she is two whole years older than Rosie. What does Grandma always say? She has to set an *example*.

Grandma has pulled out the old piano stool she's repurposed as a seat in front of the bedroom dresser and sits down. She's taking her time. She pushes her perm back from her forehead and Kezia watches, knowing the ritual. The girls have seen the routine before. Hair in place, lace coverlet on the top of the dresser neat and tidy, bedspread smooth and free of dimples left by bottoms. The jewellery box is an event. One should not open it in an untidy room or with an untidy person.

Grandma hates untidiness. That's why she doesn't visit Grandad's allotment. The roiling snakes-nest of strawberry plants and beans, and the squash of lettuces and radishes growing haphazardly around the plot distress her. On the rare occasion she makes it across the road and through the gate to the allotment, she clicks her tongue, its sharp red tip touching the front of her dentures, and she stands with her hands on her hips with a bewildered look. She doesn't ask how Grandad grows the salad he fetches most evenings, only thanks him and makes tea. Kezia has even seen her close her eyes tight when moving down the washing line, past the ramshackle greenhouse with panes of glass slipping over each other like playing cards. The garden and allotment are Grandad's. The house is hers.

As is their bedroom. She makes cushions in the evenings when the girls are asleep. She sits with Grandad in the parlour and sews fat strips of ribbon together to make the cushion covers, the stitching so perfect it is invisible, so neat it is though the ribbon has been glued together by wild alchemy. Three of these cushions lie on top of the bed in their room. A blue one, an orange one and, Kezia's favourite, one in different shades of brown. She likes the way the colours remind her of the soil at the allotment, the varying crusts of clay and earth, like the remnants of digestion.

Grandma opens the jewellery box and Rosie gasps. The ballerina springs to attention and starts to pirouette. Her tiny pink tutu twirls. She arches and, with a juddering sweep that Kezia likes best of all because it isn't quite perfect, swings her arms up and down. Grandma told them ages ago that the music is 'Greensleeves', written by an actual king –

Harry or something – and that he wrote it for a wife he later chopped the head off. Rosie had squeaked but Kezia had been thrilled. For the week after, she'd mumbled the tune in the garden and once, when she knew Grandma was in the toilet and not washing up at the kitchen window, chopped the heads off a spray of gerberas near the compost heap.

They wait, as always, for the ballerina to stop dancing and the music to stop. Rosie bounces from foot to foot and seems to strain in her dress – Kezia knows she is desperate for the ballerina to dance again but today Kezia wants to see what Grandma will choose. For she's opening the jewellery box for a special reason and not to pass time and keep the girls entertained.

'Now, I do have something in mind,' Grandma says. Her voice sounds odd. It's softer. In the kitchen she talks quickly and sounds like Kezia's old teacher, but now it's different. She sounds like she sounded when the girls first came to stay, when they couldn't sleep and Rosie threw tantrums. She spoke as if a film had come over her throat and she was talking through glass.

Grandma reaches for the middle drawer, the one she keeps bracelets in. Despite herself, Kezia leans forward to see.

Rosie practically jumps onto Grandma's knee and for once Grandma doesn't complain that she's getting too big. Instead she adjusts on the stool and lets Rosie's weight settle.

'I wonder if you know which one I'm thinking of?' she

says. 'Kezia, why don't you have a think, too?'

Kezia leans against her and now her nose is full of old lady perfume and onions. Grandma has been making stew. She's washed her hands at the kitchen sink several times, scrubbing her fingers with the rough blue soap that reminds Kezia of the tablets she's seen in pub urinals, but the smell lingers. She looks at the bracelets and tries to ignore it. She hates stew.

'That one, Grandma?' Rosie is pointing to a bracelet made of white beads. Every three bead or so there is a blue one. Grandma picks it up.

'You do like that one, don't you?' She laughs. 'Cheap little thing. Your Grandad bought it for me on our first holiday to Skegness after your Mum left home. Less than a pound at the market next to the hotel. No, we need to send something a bit fancier.'

'Why not give her a ring, Grandma?' Kezia asks.

Grandma smiles, but Kezia can see it's not a real smile. It's as if she's painted it on, as if the faces Rosie draws on the art-pad Grandad picked up in town have been traced onto her mouth. 'Andy has already given her a ring, I expect.'

This is why they are here, looking at Grandma's jewellery box. Uncle Andy, a mythical figure living on his head in Australia, has met a lady, started courting, and now they are getting married. *Melinda*. Kezia has never heard a name like that before. When Grandad read Andy's letter aloud – because Grandma couldn't and was sitting in the armchair, making strange gulping noises – Kezia heard the name like a thump to the head. No one she knew or saw on the telly or at the shops with Grandad was called *Melinda*.

And then Kezia had felt a flame in her chest. They would be friends! Uncle Andy's new wife and she – they would be pen pals! The shared weirdness of their names and the fact that they'd never find pencils or badges with their names pre-printed would unite them! But then Grandad read on and Andy had said Melinda wasn't that unusual name for Australia. The flame died a little, but Kezia still holds out hope.

'What does *Melinda's* ring look like, Grandma?' she asks, wistfully.

'Oh, I don't know. I couldn't see on the photograph Andy sent. Too blurry.'

'What about this one instead?' and Rosie has dived in, desperate to touch the bracelets because this is never allowed, and she scoops out a rope of glass.

Grandma takes it from her and holds it on her palm. Sunlight streams through the bedroom window and rounds out the glass spheres, turning them thunderously purple and blue. Kezia holds her breath.

'Maybe. Good choice, Rosie. You have an eye for this.'

Kezia bristles, for this is not how compliments should be ordered. They should roll downwards towards Rosie, sieved through Kezia. What a lovely picture you've drawn, Kezia, and thank you Rosie for helping. You've done a good job of polishing Grandad's shoes, Kezia, and thank you Rosie

31

for finding the rags under the sink. Kezia moves closer and picks up the first bracelet within reach.

It is a red one, deep garnet, the colour of old blood. The stones are fat and heavy. Kezia dangles it from her fingers and a memory buds inside, curling back like a flower. Standing in a shop with her mother. Another person was there, but it wasn't Dad. And yet he held her hand and, with the other, she thinks he touched Mum in the small of her back.

Grandma swallows. Her dentures creak. She looks at Kezia and takes the bracelet. Rosie has started to touch the ballerina, oblivious.

'This one, Kezia?' Grandma asks.

Kezia shrugs. There are gold links between the stones, the colour of yolk. Another memory rises; setting at a table with white flowers in a vase, Mum and the strange man on either side of her while she dips a soldier into an egg. She thinks they had been at a hotel. 'It looks expensive.'

'It is.' Grandma's smile has slipped upside down. She looks the way she does when she reads a horrible story in the newspapers with the red tops. Maybe the bracelet reminds her of them? Kezia thinks.

Grandma places the glass bracelet and the red one on the dresser. She slips Rosie from her lap, leaving the girl to stroke the ballerina's tutu, and moves to the bed. She pats the bedspread next to her and Kezia sits down. Grandma opens her body and hugs her in, and Kezia snuggles. She's still little enough to fit perfectly under Grandma's armpit and rests her head against her neck. She wears a pink tabard, as usual, and it also smells of onions.

'I expect you know who that bracelet belongs to, Kezia,' Grandma says, softly.

Kezia squeezes her eyes shut.

'She gave it to me for safe keeping. A few other things, too. They are for you and Rosie. She'll sort through everything when, when…'

'When she comes back?'

'Yes.' Grandma's arm stiffens and she wedges Kezia closer. Kezia feels her nuzzle the top of her head and sigh. A warm blast of hair on Kezia's scalp, like a bird settling on a nest. 'So you see, Kezia, it's lovely of you to think of giving the bracelet to Melinda, but it's yours. Or Rosie's.'

'Melinda might like it, Grandma.' For some reason there are tears coming and Kezia feels ashamed. She tries to hold them back, feels them gather in her eyelashes, and keeps as still as she can so they don't spill down her face. All she knows is she doesn't want the bracelet, though she doesn't know why.

'I'm sure Melinda would. But imagine the cost of sending it all the way to Australia. Kezia, think of all those stamps!' Grandma speaks brightly, but she's forcing it. She doesn't know how to be funny. Grandad is the joker, holding out his finger for the girls to pull when he's about to fart, swinging them on the allotment gate and, once, putting his dentures in Rosie's glass of milk. Grandma can't tell a joke to save her life.

But Kezia loves her very much at that moment and wraps her arms around her waist. Her tears splash onto the tabard and plop onto the folds in Grandma's lap.

'Maybe Andy will send me a new photograph, of Melinda wearing whatever bracelet we send,' Grandma says.

Kezia sniffs. 'Do you miss him?'

Rosie stops playing with the ballerina and turns round. Her face is a sharp little arrow and Kezia feels her unhappiness. It's not a question they are supposed to ask, just like they know not to touch Grandad's pocketknife or turn on the gas fire, or stroke Missy when she's eating. Small but immoveable rules, a wire frame over the house.

Kezia swings her legs and her sandal catches the edge of something under the bed. She knows what it is. Andy's letters, when he remembers to write, are bundles of gems landing on the doormat and Grandma and Grandad read them for days. There is a special shoe box under the bed that Grandma thinks Kezia doesn't know about, where the letters are stored. Pieces of a person kept in a blue Jonathan James box.

Rosie moves to the bed, to the other side of Grandma. They make a wonky triangle sitting together.

'Very much. Andy has a lovely life over there.' Grandma says, eventually. 'All that sun.'

'And cow poo,' Rosie shudders. She still hasn't forgotten Andy's words about cattle on the ranch.

Grandma laughs. 'Well, Melinda doesn't seem to mind. She works on the ranch, too.'

'Does she ride a horse?' Rosie's eyes are wide. 'Like on *Bonanza*?'

'Idiot,' Kezia mutters.

'Be nice,' Grandma warns. 'I don't know, Rosie. Maybe.'

'So, you miss him?' Kezia twists her fingers on her lap. The question, and the answer to it, feels terribly important to her. Grandad's calendar, a freebie from the *Mirror* newspaper, is pinned to the kitchen wall next to the orange clock, and he crosses off dates as they pass. Mum's been away for twenty-seven days.

Kezia knows she misses her; she knows the feeling of heat in her belly that flares whenever Mum is mentioned comes from her being *Not There*, but there's something else. Some mornings Kezia doesn't want to get up. She rolls over into the warm space left by Rosie, who is already downstairs eating her Weetabix, having taken the cream from the top of the milk, but on those mornings Kezia doesn't care even about that outrage. Her world is grey. Her body feels heavy. *Not There* is like an old cat, claws in her shoulder, pushing her down.

But Grandma knows *Not There* as well and she seems okay. Andy and Mum are both *Not There*. Does it hurt more when your child is away rather than your Mum? But Grandma's mum died and is away too. Kezia knows this, she's seen the photograph above the fireplace in the parlour, of a woman in a dress below her shins and ugly shoes, blinking angrily into the camera. How can Grandma get up every day when her mum is permanently *Not There*?

Grandma sighs. She slips an arm around Rosie and hugs both girls. She's still strong. She can lift a full basket of wet washing, no problem, though the way she holds damp sheets in her teeth while pegging out makes Kezia wince.

'Of course I miss him, Kezia. We all miss people we love very much when they aren't here. I bet you miss your mum. I miss her too. But she's away sorting things out.'

'Mum is coming back, isn't she?' Rosie, sounding small.

'Don't you worry, she'll be back at the end of the holidays, just like she promised. Andy though – well, he has his life in Australia. He's getting married and might have children. You'll have cousins.'

'Australian cousins?' The thought makes Kezia sit up. *Australian cousins?* She can't imagine it. 'Would we ever see them?'

'I hope so.' Grandma sniffs. Then she gives the girls one last squeeze. 'Right.' They both know that 'right.' It's a full stop. Kezia and Rosie are about to be organised. 'It's too nice a day to be stuck in here. Rosie, I'll send Melinda the bracelet you picked out. Just imagine that hot sun catching the glass. Come on, outside with you both. Grandad's in the greenhouse and needs help picking tomatoes.'

Rosie slides from the bed happily and is already thumping down the stairs by the time Grandma stands up. Rosie likes the greenhouse, especially the old water spray that looks like a musket.

Kezia takes her time. Her throat feels scratchy as if she might cry again. She hopes Grandma hasn't noticed.

Grandma is standing at the dresser now, putting the blood-red bracelet back on its tray.

'I know it's hard for you to understand what your mum is doing right now, Kezia,' Grandma says softly, without turning round. 'It's hard for me too, so goodness knows what you must be thinking. But she will be back. She just has a few things to decide.'

'In Germany?' The words are out before she can stop them and Kezia brings a hand to her mouth. She hadn't meant to say. That she knows that Mum is in Germany is her deepest secret this summer, almost as big as the one she kept from her teachers about Rosie's arm. She heard Grandma and Grandad talking in the parlour one night when she should have been asleep.

Grandma stills. Kezia sees her fingers tremble. She is touching the bracelet. The smell of onions gets stronger, and Kezia realises with a feeling of sadness that Grandma is sweating.

'Yes,' Grandma says. Then she closes the jewellery box. It snaps shut with a loud click like the sound Kezia heard in her own head, the time she fell off her bike and bit into her tongue. Grandma smooths down her tabard. 'I think Grandad's calling you. Will you see if Missy needs more water when you go down? Poor old thing doesn't do well in this heat.'

There is really nothing more to say and Kezia knows the finality that comes over Grandma at times, as sure as when she puts on her slippers and rollers in her hair. When she appears in those while Kezia and Rosie are eating their supper just before bed, they know she's done for the day - no more drinks or snacks, no more stories. She's going to sit in front of *Wogan* in the parlour and have a glass of port.

But, as Kezia pads slowly down the stairs, she leaves Grandma behind, and when she's out in the garden and looks up at the house, she sees Grandma at the bedroom window and her hand is over her face.

The Storm

It has been raining for three days. Fat, heavy bulbs of water, spilling from a black sky. And now lightning. Angry white flashes, accompanied by a noise that sounds like the piano in the parlour has fallen over. The sky fills with silver and gardens are lit up. Sheds and swings and chicken coops become crackling black shapes, alien and unfamiliar. A moment of stillness, a holding breath into which the hall clock ticks once, twice.

Rosie jumps so many times she is exhausted, and Grandad eventually settles her by the gas fire. Missy, the stinky old dog, lies down next to her.

Grandad frets about his allotment. The beans are almost ready to pick. He's nurtured them, tying back vines that threaten to choke them. He won't let rabbits get them - they've eaten rabbit three times in the past week, snapped in two within their skin by Grandad's traps. Little lives ended swiftly. He guts them in his shed and they appear in Grandma's stew pot at teatime.

Grandad stalks by the window, back to the kitchen table, leaning forward over the sink to strain through the glass, muttering.

Even Grandma has enough eventually. 'Bernard, sit down! There's nothing you can do.'

Grandad flicks on the kettle and sits down with a whoosh of air. The weather brings out the ache in his hip. He can't get comfortable on the Formica chairs around the kitchen table and Missy is now on the armchair. Her hips are worse than Grandad's. Kezia knows he doesn't have the heart to turf her off the seat.

'What makes thunder and lightning, Grandad?' Rosie mumbles from the rug. Her thumb is in her mouth. She hasn't done that for weeks.

'Oh, I don't know.' Grandad grins. 'Something to do with electricity.'

'We did it at school before the summer,' Kezia says. She's got her box of felt-tips out and is at the table, drawing a storm on an oval of cardboard. Grandma has a stash of them, lids from boxes of tissues. Grandma's nose is always running. Kezia likes the shape of the lids. They remind her of cameo brooches like the ones worn by posh ladies on black and white films. 'It's when cold air and warm air rub together.'

'Is that so, Kezia?' Grandad says admiringly. 'Well, well, the things they teach you at school these days.'

Kezia shrugs. Her belly groans. Grandma made broth and dumplings for lunch and she's eaten too much. She couldn't stop. Dumplings are my terrible weakness, she thinks, remembering the princess on the film they watched the night before, who was kept apart from her penniless boyfriend by a cruel governess. *He is my terrible weakness.* Kezia had felt all shivery when the poor princess had said that. Not even jewels or feasts or the offer of marriage from a handsome but obviously villainous count could sway the lady. On the oval of cardboard, Kezia starts to draw a castle against the backdrop of the storm.

'I left school at fourteen,' Grandad says. His fretfulness about his beans makes him talkative. The girls know this fact about Grandad that he didn't *have much in the way of schooling*, for it was said by their Dad said many times. Kezia remembers Dad standing in their kitchen at home, still wearing his work suit even though he'd been home for hours. He was angry about something. He said that thing about Grandad and his mouth was a weird, twisted line.

She looks up, suddenly sorry for Grandad, and pats his arm. She doesn't know what to say. He smiles at her but not with his eyes and she can see he's over at his allotment, among the twisted roots and weeds and the slight smell of cat piss.

'Why did you leave at fourteen, Grandad?' Rosie asks. She's taken her thumb from her mouth and is now winding her hair around her fingers. Kezia's belly throbs dangerously. Rosie's hair will stink of spit, an awful, sweet smell that reminds Kezia of the gum on envelopes. It's not bath night. Kezia's going to smell her all night, for Rosie always curls herself round her sister in her sleep, even when Kezia rolls to the other end of the bed.

'That was what happened when we were young,' Grandma says. 'I left school at thirteen.'

This bit is news. It's delightful to find out something new about Grandma. She's a curved map and they think they know her, all the dimples and folds on her jaw, and the strange bend to her knuckles when the weather is cold. They know every woollen cardigan and bobbled pair of tights and sour-smelling slippers. But they didn't know this.

Rosie gets up from the rug and swings an arm over Grandma's neck. She's very tired. Another crack in the sky outside and she perches on Grandma's lap. 'I'd like to not go to school again,' she sighs.

'Oh no, chicken, you wouldn't. I wanted to stay on. But it was different when your Grandad and I were little. Bernard, I think that kettle has boiled.' Grandma watches Grandad pour water into the silver teapot. 'But there were eight of us children. I had to help my mother.'

'Tracy at school has four big brothers,' Kezia says. Her voice is an oyster of wonder. So many brothers seems impossible.

'I had four as well,' Grandad says. He's patting the teapot already, impatient for a brew. 'And five sisters.'

'So that's…' Rosie counts on her fingers. 'Nine of you?'

'Ten,' Kezia corrects her smugly. She knew that already. Mum drew a map of them once, though she couldn't remember all their names. Kezia remembers the sheet of paper on the dining table, lines between them like spider legs. Names and no-names connected to each other, wired together. Another flash in the sky, a big one this time, and they all jump. Grandad slops tea from the pot and he gets up, apologetic glance at Grandma, and wipes up the mess with the dishcloth.

'Did you have a big house?' Rosie asks. 'Or a castle?'

Kezia groans. 'Oh, don't be stupid.'

'Now Kezia, that's a fair question.' Grandad grins, and Kezia knows he's about to come out with one of his high tales. She giggles. She can't help herself, though her tummy still hurts and Rosie is so *thick* sometimes. But she loves Grandad's fibs.

Grandad pours a mug of tea for him and fills Grandma's china cup, with the faded pink roses, and leans back. He's preparing himself. 'I wouldn't describe it as a castle. More a country manor. Like that place we went to last year for...' he stumbles and Kezia sees he realises he's made a mistake, '...for your mother's birthday.'

Grandma snorts.

'Did you have servants?' Rosie's eyes are buttons.

'Oh, dozens. Servants to sweep and dust and keep the place tidy, servants to light fires – no gas fires in those days, girls! – servants to make our meals.' Grandad winks. 'The only thing we didn't have a servant for was for that thing Henry VIII got them to do.'

'Henry VIII?' Rosie says.

'Big fat king. Had six wives and chopped the head off two. Bet you'll learn about him at school as well, eh Kezia?'

Kezia smiles widely, delighted at the authority Grandad lay on her. 'He wrote the music that plays in Grandma's jewellery box.'

'That's right! Well, the important thing to remember is that Henry was a huge bugger,' Grandad says, sweeping his hands around his own pot-belly. Grandma tuts at the swear word, but he carries on. His fib has life to it, he's following the line of the story, up and down its detail. 'He liked his food. Feasts and huge joints of meat, cakes and pies. Lord, he was greedy.'

'Did you meet him, Grandad?' Rosie breathes.

Grandad closes his eyes briefly. 'I believe my father did. But he was so fat he had a servant to do one particular job for him. Can you guess what it was?'

Both girls shake their head. Kezia's learned the rhyme at school about Henry – *Divorced, Beheaded, Died. Divorced, Beheaded, Survived* – but not about his use of servants. Again, fresh news on this jagged day.

'He needed a poor maid to –' Grandad pauses for effect and then suddenly gets up and bends over – 'to wipe his arse!' He shakes his sagging rump over the table.

Kezia gasps and drops her felt-tip, and then laughs. She laughs very hard, as if her own head will roll off and, indeed, holds her temples.

But Rosie doesn't laugh. Instead her eyes fill with tears and she buries her face in Grandma's neck. She cries onto Grandma's tabard. 'I don't want to do that!'

'Oh Rosie, it's just your Grandad being silly,' and Grandma pats her on the head. She shoots Grandad an exasperated look, though he's sitting down again and raising his mug of tea to his lips, a look of triumph plastered over his face.

Kezia stops laughing and glares at Rosie in annoyance. Her little sister has a strange reaction to things at times and it's *maddening*. Once they had to turn off the Tarzan film when a baddie was trapped in quicksand. Rosie had started shrieking and lifting her feet from the carpet.

'Rosie,' she says tersely. But Rosie has recovered a bit and lets Grandma hug her close. She pops her thumb back in her mouth and Kezia can see that, before long, she'll be asleep.

A distant rumble and Grandad looks out of the window. 'Storm seems to be moving off,' he says hopefully. 'Give it another hour and I'll go and check my beans.'

'Can I come, Grandad?' Kezia asks. She picks up her felt-tip and, next to the castle, starts to draw a stickman with a crown. She makes him bend at the middle, so he's leaning forward. Henry VIII will keep her giggling for a while, but the day will soon become boring again. Even the allotment and helping Grandad pick his veg is better than staying inside for another day.

'Of course you can.'

Rosie is so tired she doesn't even object or ask to come too.

'Let's put you upstairs for a nap, sweetheart,' Grandma says. Rosie's too old to be having regular naps, but she slips from Grandma's knee without a mumble and Kezia hears her stumble up the stairs. Grandma goes with her, a hand on Rosie's shoulder, rounding her through the door and to the steps so the girl doesn't drunkenly bang her head on the bannister. They hear the girls' bed creak and Grandma whispering, and then the door closing softly. Grandma pads stiffly down the stairs and sits down at the kitchen table again. She picks up her china cup with a sigh.

Then Grandad says another strange thing. He's still looking out of the window but his eyes have gone out of focus. His jaw moves silently at first and then he speaks in a rush.

'Seems about right though, Edith, a storm today. It rained that day, too. Didn't it?'

The china cup bangs against Grandma's teeth and Kezia looks up at the sound. There's an expression on the old woman's face that she hasn't seen before. Grandma puts her cup down on its saucer. There is a slight tremble to her fingers.

'Yes,' she says, barely audible.

'I've been thinking about her.' Grandad seems to be talking to himself. 'She'd be thirty today. Ah, well.'

Grandma raises a shaky hand to her face and pushes blotched fingers against her eyes. Kezia stares. When Grandma drops her hand she sees that her fingers are wet. Grandma's crying? Kezia's head swivels back and forth, between Grandad and Grandma, appalled. She's also confused. Who are they talking about?

'I remember the storm when they took her away. Such a little bundle. She had all her fingers and toes, I saw that. Just too small. Ah, well, we were luckier than most, I suppose. At least we got to see her.' Grandad's glassy voice, so dreamy and odd. Kezia can't believe he hasn't got up, to see to Grandma. This is a man who sprinted down the garden path when Grandma was pruning back the bushes and caught her finger on a rose thorn. She'd only given a little cry, but Grandad heard it, the way a dog hears a whistle, and he'd hurried his gammy hips to her. He hates to see her in pain.

But he's not even noticed Grandma is crying. His mind is far away. Another flash of lightning, upending the day. The air feels stuffy in the kitchen.

Then, because it's always Grandma, she sniffs and pats the table. 'Right,' she mutters. 'Let's go and see what there is on the telly, shall we? We can't sit boiling here all day and getting maudlin.'

Kezia is very confused, even more so at the suggestion of day-time telly, but it's such an unexpected treat that she doesn't argue. She starts to pack away her felt-tips. Upstairs, Rosie moans and rolls over. Grandma gets up and goes over to the sink, tipping the dregs of tea down the plug, and leans over the metal draining board. Then, slowly, blinking rapidly, Grandad also gets up and stands beside her. His shoulder touches hers and they watch as another splinter of light renders the sky.

The Phone Call

The girls are waiting for Mum to call. It seems like they've been waiting for days. Grandma won't let them go to the allotment with Grandad in case they miss her, though given how quiet the street is, Kezia thinks they'll be able to hear the phone ring from the allotment gate. Everyone has gone on holiday. Ferret Jack next door, the neighbour who has five ferrets that he keeps in a run in his garden, has gone to Skegness. Mrs Almond from number seven is visiting her sister at Great Yarmouth. Even Ivor at the Bottle Shop on the corner has closed up for a few days, and someone said he'd hopped on a flight to Majorca. *Hopped on a flight to Majorca* – the phrase seems outrageously exotic to Kezia. It adds a layer to the world she enters at night, when Rosie's asleep and curled around her back. *I'm sorry, Prince Julian, I cannot marry you for I have to hop on a flight to Majorca, to visit my true love, Simon le Bon.*

Grandma and Grandad aren't taking the girls away. This is a sad fact that Kezia has come to accept. The likes of a package holiday to Spain isn't for them. Kezia wonders if Grandma has ever been abroad at all. Grandad must have, for he was in the navy during the war. Sometimes he mentions Egypt. There's a paper mache mummy on the mantelpiece in the parlour, which Grandma once said he'd posted her as a gift.

No, a holiday involving a plane is unlikely to happen but,

at the start of the holidays, Kezia hoped for *something*. Even a day trip somewhere, eating warm tomato sandwiches on a train, dabbling her feet in frothy brown seawater. One day she'd found a leaflet next to the phone about short breaks at the Derbyshire Miner's Holiday Village at Skeggy, and spent the next two days breathless. But no announcement came and the leaflet disappeared.

Rosie doesn't seem to care that they haven't gone on holiday. She's still not over Andrew and Fergie's wedding. They'd watched it all day, all of them, in the parlour. Grandma made a plate of potted meat sandwiches and Grandad bought a bottle of cherry pop for the girls. They watched Fergie bounce down the aisle in her satin dress, not quite white, and Andrew in his medals. The Queen and her mother, even Margaret, dressed in blue. Rosie lay on the carpet in front of the telly, Missy beside her, and drew endlessly, filling every sheet of paper she had, with dresses and crowns and wonky horses dragging wonky carriages. Then Grandad brought home a Fergie dressing-up book of paper dolls from the newsagent. Rosie has played with it so much the folds attaching dresses to dolls have torn, and Grandma's had to fix them with Sellotape.

Grandma is washing and chopping beans from Grandad's allotment. There is a glut of them, rescued after the storm, and Kezia has come to loathe the sight. Green beans with fish, green beans with slices of meat, green beans with Sunday dinner. Tonight it will be beans with rabbit, the latest caught on the allotment. Kezia tries not to think of the small furry body, thrashing around in one of Grandad's traps, and the dark pink of its flesh when it's been skinned. The trouble is, Kezia likes the taste of rabbit, especially the way Grandma cooks it. When she's eating, she tells herself she's eating something different – a tasty, goblin-like creature who lives on the moon and really wants to be sacrificed and eaten by better people on earth.

Grandad's over at the allotment right now. He's taken Grandma's washing basket as he's hopeful of raspberries.

'Can I come?' Kezia had asked, and Rosie had jumped up from her seat at the kitchen table.

'Me too!'

Grandad had looked wistful and cast a glance at Grandma. 'Sorry girls. Your mum is calling, remember? Won't that be nice?'

'Rubbish,' Kezia had retorted and then felt ashamed when she saw Grandad's disappointed look. But he has no clue, really, how she feels about Mum phoning to speak to them.

So now Grandad is at the allotment, Grandma is at the sink, and Rosie is drawing another new dress for her paper doll. She's found a purple felt-tip, one she thought she'd lost, and everything at the moment has to be purple. Kezia scowls at her. She jabs out an elbow and Rosie's hand, adding amethyst jewels to the dress collar, shoots across the page.

'Kezia!' she squeals. Tears, immediately. 'Look what you've done!'

'What's happening, girls?'

'Nothing, Grandma!' Kezia says, exaggeratedly. 'Green beans again?'

Grandma pauses and puts down the blunt knife on the draining board. She turns and fixes Kezia with narrow eyes. 'You've been a little snippy today, young lady. I don't care for it.'

Kezia tosses her head but she cannot completely hide her deflation. She's felt, over the past week or so that she and Grandma had come to see each other as equals. Friends, almost, comrades at war, just like the soldiers in the film they watched after tea the other night. Grandma had sniffed a bit and couldn't look at Grandad. When Kezia handed her a tissue, Grandma had nodded a thank-you in a way that Kezia felt was loaded with meaning. And they shared another look when Grandad mentioned his brother Albert, lost at Dunkirk.

But, apparently Kezia has been deceived. Grandma is still very much her Grandma.

'Can I ask something, Grandma?' she asks quietly.

Grandma sighs and turns back to the beans. 'Of course.'

'Do you think – do you think we'll go on holiday this summer?'

Rosie looks up. She's interested in the answer. This surprises Kezia. Rosie starts to doodle a violet flower on the edge of her paper.

Grandma turns round again and this time wipes her hands on the tea towel. There is a finality to the movement.

'We won't, Kezia.'

'What about Skegness?' Rosie asks. She bobs her head onto her shoulder and Kezia can see she's torn. She must have seen the leaflet as well. The heated swimming pool at the Miner's Welfare was a killer.

Grandma comes and sits at the table. She presses her palm down flat on the surface, fingers still slightly wet from the sink. The nails are shiny and pink, like the inside of a shell. 'It would be very nice, of course. But we can do the things we'd do at Skegness here! We'll play bingo tonight, how about that?'

Kezia and Rosie share a glance and look down at the table. Bingo in the parlour! It won't be the same at all as being on holiday. Kezia feels angry.

'Is it because you're giving money to Roy's son?' she blurts out. The words fall from her like bombs, they splinter at Grandma's feet and throw debris into the old lady's face. Grandma flinches. A tiny movement, but the girls see it. Her shoulders roll forwards.

'What do you know about Roy's son?' she asks quietly.

Kezia hesitates. Grandma's initial reaction is one she's used to – she's seen Mum adjust her body to receive and cushion words thrown at her that might cause pain. Sometimes, in the days of *before*, Kezia got up at night when Mum and Dad were rowing; she sat halfway down the stairs, wrapped in shadow, and watched Mum standing in the kitchen, arms clamped to her sides, suddenly folding herself together like the Jacob's ladder Grandad made, as Dad threw words at her. Grandma – Mum's Mum, after all – reacts just the same. Her body has coiled around the words. Now Kezia feels bad.

'I've just heard things, that's all,' she says. She's aware her voice is shaking. Rosie looks at her curiously. 'It's nothing.'

'No, I suppose it's natural for you to be interested. Your Grandad and I are not good at sneaking around.' Grandma smiles sadly.

'I wasn't trying to listen, honest,' Kezia says quickly, but they both know it's not true. Grandma strokes Kezia's hair, enough pressure in her fingers to tell the girl to stop lying.

'Roy's son is a solicitor,' Grandma says. 'Hard to believe – I remember him coming round here to play soldiers with Andy, but there you are. Always was clever and got a grant to go to university. I'd hoped your Mum might have done the same but – ah well, it doesn't matter.'

'Are you in trouble, Grandma?' Kezia asks. She's heard the word *solicitor* before, on *The Bill*. A little ribbon of panic starts to flutter inside – what if Grandad kills too many rabbits at the allotment and has to spend *a night in the cells*? The thought of telling her friends when she goes back to school, about her jailbird Grandad, is thrilling and mortifying.

But Grandad - and Grandma, for that matter – aren't in any trouble. 'Of course not, Kezia.' Grandma looks at Rosie, dramatically engrossed in drawing a purple crown for her paper doll, and they both know she is listening hard. 'Roy's son – he's called Stephen – specialises in Family Law.'

'What's Family Law?' Kezia hears the capital letters and repeats them. She imagines a big *F* and a big *L* rising from the carpet like credits on the black and white films they watch every day.

But Grandma's closing up. Her mouth purses, the conversation is about to end. 'That's for another day,' she says. 'Don't you worry about it. And I'm sorry. There won't be a holiday this year.'

The anger returns. Kezia knows Mum thinks she was upset and frightened by the rows and then the heavy cloud that descended whenever Mum and Dad were in the same room, but actually Kezia came to resent the clamming up more. The abrupt cutting off of words when she entered a room made her feel as if she'd stepped onto the edge of a cliff. She'd wander into the kitchen and Mum and Dad would close their mouths, sometimes with a little click, and Kezia would feel immediate panic. Grown-ups believe they are protecting us, but they're making it worse, she thinks.

'What if Dad sent you some money?' she asks suddenly. 'I know you have his phone number. You could get Grandad to ask him.'

Grandma is incredibly still. 'No, Kezia.'

'Why not?' Kezia feels spiteful. She knows why not, even though she's never said the words out loud or heard her Grandma say them. Grandma *hates* Dad. Since Christmas.

Kezia hates all kinds of things and occasionally people, but it's an emotion that is transient and as impermanent as the static that clouds the television screen when it is first switched on. The feeling grips her terribly at the start and is focused liked a dart – Rosie has spent too long in the bath again, so the water is cold when Kezia gets in; that awful girl, Lucy, who they met at the chip shop and who asked too many questions and didn't seem to breathe when she spoke – but then certainty melts away. It is like vinegar, tart and curling on her tongue, but gone as soon as she swallows.

Still, it is unsettling to think that Grandma has such feelings. Grandma cries when she reads the newspaper and some child has disappeared or died horribly, and then doesn't let the girls out of her sight for a few hours – she doesn't seem a person capable of hate. But she is, and Kezia is certain of it, and the fact the object of such emotion is her father doesn't surprise her at all.

Then the phone rings and Grandma – or maybe Kezia, she isn't sure – is rescued. Grandma gets up and they hear her speak into the handset. Rosie leans over to Kezia.

'I think it's Mum.'

It must be. Grandma's voice has done that weird thing again, as if she's holding her feelings in her throat. She sounds like she's sucked helium from a balloon. *Yes, they are both fine. Of course, twice a week. Rosie doesn't like the shampoo so we got her something different. Sleeping ok now, yes. How are things...out there?*

Kezia holds her breath. She strains every part of her body to hear the conversation in the hallway. On the wall the old railway clock ticks and she feels the beat in her mouth. She clamps it between her teeth, grinding gums together.

Something within her is praying for words that will make sense of this summer and why they are at Grandma's house. She isn't listening to Grandma out of nosiness, not completely. Tightness spreads down her jaw and into the fine bones of her neck and she thinks she might snap with the weight of sudden, pressing longing for her mother.

Grandma calls them and Rosie is first to slip from her chair and thunder down the hall. She squeaks into the phone, not making any sense, and everything spills from her five-year-old body in a rush.

Kezia doesn't move. She realises she needs the toilet really badly. Strange, she hadn't felt it before, but now her bladder feels pinkly swollen, like an udder on one of the cows they sometimes see in the fields beyond the allotments. Grandma walks slowly into the kitchen and stands beside her. She drops a hand on Kezia's shoulder and the air the girl had been holding in her chest surrenders in a burst.

'Kezia!' Rosie hollers. She sounds impossibly happy. 'Mum doesn't have many coins left!'

Kezia gets up and walks to the phone, which seems miles away. She looks at the wallpaper and the frames lining the hallway. Grandad in his navy uniform, Grandma as a Wren. Andy and Mum as children, standing next to their grandmother who looked like a thinner, angrier version of Grandma. Kezia wants this moment of *before* to last, this holding moment before she takes the handset from her sister and hears her mother's voice for the first time in days.

If she can slow down time now, maybe she can slow down time when she speaks to Mum, all those miles away.

But Rosie is waving the phone at her frantically, close enough to swipe her nose, and Kezia has to grab it.

'Hello,' she says, softly.

A pause, a beat longer than the delay on the connection, and her Mum's voice fills her ear. 'There's my little egg.'

Mum's name for her. Apparently her belly looked like a brown hen's egg when she was pregnant with Kezia, so that's what she calls her baby. Kezia both likes and dislikes it. Rosie doesn't have a nickname, though sometimes Mum calls her *rosebud* – but that's not really a nickname, just an extension of her real, actual name. Kezia doesn't think it counts. She told Rosie it doesn't count. But then Rosie started holding her nose and saying eggs stink like farts, so now Kezia isn't sure she likes her own nickname at all.

No one has called her a little egg for almost a month. Kezia's determined to feel cross at Mum but now finds she can't. The static of hate has cleared away, so rapidly.

'Mummy,' is all she can say, helplessly.

'Are you crying? Oh, don't cry. I miss you too. So much, Kezia.'

Mum's voice is muffled by the line. Kezia can hear voices in the background, and the noise of plates being moved or stacked. A blast of steam like the sound a machine makes when warming milk. She thinks Mum is in a café. 'What are you doing?'

'I'm just out. Seeing friends, you know.' Mum is talking

quickly. Kezia listens hard to the sounds bookending Mum's voice and she can't make out what people are saying. She thinks *Germany*.

'When are you coming home?'

Hundreds of miles away, Mum sighs. Kezia imagines her holding the handset close to her body, curling it into her shoulder, the way she used to speak into the phone in the weeks after Dad left. Sometimes Kezia would come downstairs at night when she should be in bed, the telly still blaring, and Mum would be on the sofa talking to someone on the phone. Her feet would be tucked under her bottom, her hair still damp from the bath, and the handset would be close enough to her body that Kezia didn't see it at first. Instead she'd think her mum looked like a hedgehog.

'Rosie asked me the same thing. I'll be back at the end of the holidays, a few days before school.' Mum's voice is consumed by a background noise, a shout over a tannoy somewhere, and Kezia doesn't hear what she says next.

'Are you at a train station?'

'I said it won't be long, little egg.'

'Are you at a train station?'

Another pause. 'Yes.'

Kezia blinks back sudden tears. Her mum is travelling somewhere! She's away from her children and she's getting on a train to go even further. The pressure in Kezia's bladder increases and she squeezes her thighs together. She wants to say to Mum that she should take a train to come home and get them. But she doesn't say anything of the sort.

Mum is a hedgehog.

Behind her, in the kitchen, Rosie says something and Grandma laughs.

'I have to go now, Kezia,' Mum says. 'I'm sorry, it's expensive to call. But I'll ring again next week and we can have a proper chat. Okay?'

'Where are you going? Why are you getting on a train?'

Mum doesn't reply at first, and Kezia thinks that the connection has been lost. Her hand is sweaty around the handset. Has she squeezed it too hard and choked off the call? She wonders if that's how phone calls work, that they have to have space to breathe.

Then Mum replies. 'I'm going to a place called Sennelager. I'll tell you all about it when I come home. Now, be a good girl for Grandma and Grandad, won't you? I love you, little egg.'

Kezia is about to say something but the call has ended. She heard the pips – an impossibly short time – and then it's over. Sennelager? What was that? Why would Mum be going there?

Grandma calls from the kitchen. 'Kezia? Has she gone?'

And then Kezia looks down and, with a sense of deep shame, realises she has wet herself.

The Bread Poultice

It's Saturday night again – Kezia has lost count how many they've had at Grandma's house and thinks it might be three – and they are all in the parlour watching *Final Score* on the telly. Grandad is doing the Pools. He's holding a thin notepad in his hand, leaning it against his knee, and when the presenter reads out the football scores, he makes a mark on the paper in pencil, using a tiny stub kept on the mantelpiece for the very purpose. He perches on the edge of the armchair like a nervous deer.

Kezia and Rosie are supposed to be quiet while the scores are read out, for this could be Grandad's *ticket to fortune* and he needs to concentrate. He says it every week, as well as reminding them all, again, about the time he won £36.

'Paid for winter coats and new shoes for us all, didn't it love?' he says to Grandma, who has heard it all a million times before and can only bring herself to nod.

Rosie's doing her best to be quiet so Grandad can hear the announcer, but her arm is hurting her again. She's lying on the settee. A hot water bottle, one of Grandma's old porcelain ones, is wrapped in a towel and is pressed against her skin. Kezia remembers Mum telling Grandma that the bone between Rosie's elbow and shoulder has healed, but every now and then she sleeps funny, and her arm throbs all day. She sighs and moans, and Grandma rubs her forehead. There's a tight look on Grandma's face, the kind she got when helping Ferret Jack next door to patch up his fingers when one of his animals took a fancy to it.

Kezia knows Rosie's not faking it. Sometimes she fakes a tummy ache or a pain in her head, clasping herself extravagantly when it's time to tidy the room they share, or sweep the garden path of daisy chains and fairy picnics. Fairy picnics have become Rosie's thing recently. Grandma read them a story one night, an old one of Mum's, and Rosie had stared and stared at the illustration of fairies dressed in impossible lace and silk the thickness of breath, gathered around a toadstool for supper. Plates made of clover, tiny flower heads instead of cakes. There are toadstools in Grandad's garden, but the ugly kind, the colour of week-old dog shit, so Rosie uses Grandad's upturned bucket as the fairy dell. Leaves from the apple tree replace clover, but there are plenty of daisies on the front lawn, enough to make chains and feed fairies. Rosie never wants to tidy them away when it's time to come in for tea.

But she's pale and sweaty as she lies on the settee and Kezia knows her arm hurts worse than usual. She doesn't remember much about the day that it happened; memories of Rosie in a plaster cast, unable to dress herself, are stronger. Dad had left by then, so she'd helped Mum get Rosie into her school clothes. Kezia didn't mind that, but avoided helping Rosie eat at dinnertime. She is so messy.

Kezia is playing with her gypsy caravan made from an old toilet roll. It's not as sturdy and magnificent as the one she made a couple of weeks ago, from the cardboard tube

Grandad brought home from the Post Office, but Kezia tries not to think of that one. It still hurts too much. It had been her best creation yet; Grandad had bought the girls a new pack of felt-tips and so the colours on the caravan were rich and bright, and not at all faded or scrubbed like the marks their old pens left. The red around the caravan windows reminded Kezia of her mother's lipstick, and the gold leaves over the door were the colour of Dad's car. She put the Duplo man and woman in the caravan front and trundled them up and down the garden path, as if they were a married couple still in love and on holiday. Then she left the caravan outside on the day of the storm, the huge one than tore up Grandad's lettuces on the allotment, and she found the Duplo couple in a big, paper mache puddle. She'd cried all morning.

The Duplo couple are sitting in the toilet roll caravan, but they don't look happy about it. Maybe that's what real life is like, Kezia thinks.

The presenter reading out the football scores has moved onto League Two and Grandad edges forward on his chair. Kezia listens too. She and Rosie like *Final Score*. Grandad's marks on his notepad are a mystery and Kezia can't understand how a group of men playing football in a town she's never heard of could make Grandad rich, but she forgets about that when the presenter speaks. He has a way of raising or lowering his voice when saying the teams' names, so you can guess the result. If he starts off low and then lifts his voice when saying the second team's name, you know the second team has won. He has a special way of saying a match is a score or nil draw. Rosie thinks she's predicting the future when she guesses if the first team he says has won or lost, and squeaks when she gets them all right.

She isn't listening right now, though, and this is another reason Kezia knows her sister isn't faking. She wonders if Rosie will even notice when *The Dukes of Hazzard* comes on.

'That girl needs a bread poultice,' Grandad mutters. The presenter is on League Three and he's stopped writing on his pad. Kezia knows he hasn't won again. It's been the same every Saturday since they came to stay. Grandad gets twitchy from about three o'clock in the afternoon and returns from the allotment rubbing his hands. He wants a new shed, with electric, and a brand-new Bose radio and garden tools that shine like the moon. Then, at about half past four, he goes into the parlour and knocks his knuckles against every piece of wood in there – the mantelpiece, the picture frames, the old dresser. Of course, the piano. Knocking for luck, he'd wink at Kezia.

Then, when he doesn't win, he gets up and stands in the middle of the room, hands on hips, trousers held up with a piece of rope, and sighs and shakes his head.

Today, though, he lays the notepad down on the rug when the scores are all done and, silently, gets up and walks into the kitchen. Kezia stares after him. The kitchen door is open and she can see his thin frame and pot belly bustle between the sink and cupboards.

'What's he doing?' she asks.

Grandma is edging Rosie onto her side and straightening the hot water bottle. Rosie is quieter but her eyes are glassy and she doesn't seem to be looking at anything. Kezia doesn't like it and, for the first time, feels a little shiver of fear. What if a tiny piece of bone has broken off in Rosie's arm and is travelling through her body right now? It could be torpedoing through her blood, in the shape of the disgusting liquorice sweets that Grandad sometimes gets from the Bottle Shop, aiming right for her heart.

Grandma hasn't answered her and her brow is creased, thick flesh furrowed. Her expression doesn't ease Kezia's worry. Kezia leans against the settee and pushes her nose against Rosie's.

'Nose kiss, Rosebud,' she says. She thinks she might cry.

Grandma's hand drops onto Kezia's head and the old woman smooths down her hair. 'She just needs to rest, Kezia. It hurts her sometimes, that's all. Like your Grandad's hips do when it's cold.'

Grandad is clattering about with saucepans now and they hear him swear. Kezia giggles. She really hopes Rosie has heard him. Grandad has the most tremendous swears. He makes Grandma cross, but she always says it's the navy in him, and that seems to make it all right. Sometimes Kezia and Rosie whisper the swear words to each other in bed at night, sniggering almost enough to wet themselves.

Rosie seems to be drifting asleep, so Kezia gets up and goes into the kitchen to see what Grandad is doing. She finds him tearing up pieces of bread and putting them in a saucepan.

'What are you doing, Grandad?'

'Bread poultice, Kezia. Best thing to draw out the pain.' Grandad switches off the kettle just before it boils and dumps a steaming thread of water over the mess in the saucepan. 'Pass me a spoon.'

Kezia gets one from the drawer next to the cooker – one of Grandma's best ones with an ivory handle and a blue windmill painted on the top - and gives it to him. She watches, bewildered, as Grandad stirs the gloop together until it becomes a fat, doughy ball. Then, with just his fingertips, he shapes it into a flat pancake. 'This will sort her. Fellow I served with was bitten by an adder in Egypt. Same one that killed Cleopatra. The cook whipped up a bread poultice and the poison was sucked out, like a flash.'

Kezia feels warm and fuzzy inside, as if she's slipped inside a thick coat. Grandad's telling one of his tall tales again, and she loves him very much for it. 'Will it really help Rosie?'

Grandad's face becomes tight, just like Grandma's did earlier when she was trying to get Rosie to settle, and he sighs. His sleeves are rolled up so Kezia can see faded blue tattoos, and the flesh on his arms is loose and soft. He's no longer a strong man. She wonders if this bothers him. He was incredibly handsome in his navy photos from the war, with muscles that looked big enough to pull the enemy apart. Or pulverise anyone who hurt the people he loved.

'Worth a try, darling,' he says. 'Come on.'

They return to the parlour. Grandad crouches down in front of the settee with the saucepan, wincing a little as his joints pop. He touches Rosie's sore arm gently.

'Can you sit up, pet?'

'Oh Bernard, not one of those things again,' Grandma objects. She points at the saucepan and the grey, steaming bread. 'You didn't even use a bowl!'

'Rosie? Let's getting you sitting up.'

'This is ridiculous,' and Grandma is angry. She stands up and folds her arms. She's wearing her weekend tabard, the blue on with a white trim, which Kezia likes because it means roast dinners and jelly and custard in front of the telly. But, with Grandma standing there, she sees the fabric of the tabard is ripped, at the point where Grandma ties it. Kezia hasn't noticed the rip before. For a reason she can't understand, it makes her feel sad.

'It's not ridiculous, Edith,' Grandad says, indignantly.

'It saved his friend who was bitten by an adder,' Kezia offers, quietly.

Grandma says nothing but glares at Grandad.

Rosie has woken up and grumbles as Grandad helps her upright. Her face isn't quite as pale now but she still clutches her arm, just at the elbow.

'Does your elbow hurt worst of all?' Grandad asks gently, and Rosie nods. She's blinking, as if she's just broken the surface of the swimming pool after holding her breath for as long as possible. 'Right then, can you roll your sleeve up?'

'For Christ's sake, Bernard,' Grandma spits. A shocking moment. Kezia's never heard Grandma swear before, if *for Christ's sake* is even a swear word. Is it? Kezia wonders if she should ask. But Grandma's face is so angry she doesn't. She's confused. It doesn't seem right to be furious at a ball of wet bread.

Grandad helps Rosie lift up her sleeve. She's wearing a cardigan, knitted by Grandma, and it's a little tight, but eventually she gets it up to her shoulder. 'What are you doing, Grandad?' she asks.

'An old navy trick, my dear. Now, this will be hot. I want you to be brave and let me hold it against your elbow.'

'If you scald her with that thing, Bernard, I swear to God…' an unfinished threat from Grandma on this strangest of evenings.

Kezia swallows. Tears are in her throat.

Grandad picks up the bread poultice and, carefully, presses it against Rosie's elbow. It's still steaming, but not as much as in the kitchen. Rosie gasps and squirms. Grandma moves forward, and Kezia thinks for a second she's going to hit Grandad – *if she does, I'm going to throw up, right here on the rug* – but then Rosie calms and sighs. She holds the messy dough in place.

'How does that feel, my little Rosebud?' Grandad asks. His eyes are very bright.

'Really good,' Rosie says.

Grandad sits back on his heels and grins. His face is one of triumph. 'Lovely. Now you hold it there until it doesn't feel warm anymore. If you need another one, you just say to your Grandad. Midshipman Bernard Thorpe. At your service.' He does a salute.

'Must you turn everything into a game?' Grandma hisses.

'Think these girls need more games, if you ask me.' Grandad has become a little smug. Kezia's only seen him like this once before, last week, when someone called the house and she heard him say they could only *make contact through your solicitor, you absolute disgrace*, and had hung up.

He picks up the saucepan. 'I fancy a cup of tea. Kezia, why don't you sit with your sister for a spell and watch *Dukes of Hazzard*? Must be coming on soon.'

It is. It's a programme both girls love. Kezia feels awkward and her belly fills with fizz when Bo Duke comes on the screen, while Rosie wants to be Daisy. And as for the way they leap into the car...

The parlour door is left open and, despite the Hazzard theme tune coming on and Rosie nestling in beside her, Kezia listens to Grandma and Grandad as they make tea.

Grandma sits at the table. The chair squeaks. 'She needs a doctor, Bernard.'

'I know.' Grandad is filling the kettle. 'But that's for Anna to decide.'

Kezia leans a little away from Rosie so she can hear. Boss Hogg has just blustered on screen.

'Do you think she remembers any of it?' Grandma is tracing her fingers around the plastic table cloth, like she does when listening to the radio late at night.

There is the sound of water being poured into the silver pot and Grandad says something that Kezia doesn't catch. Then the scrape of a chair as he joins Grandma at the table, and he says 'she'll dream about it when she gets older.'

'Like you do, Bernie.' Grandma's voice is softer.

'Even now. Still see the lads' faces in the water.'

A silence, filled only with the sound of Boss Hogg arguing with Uncle Jesse. Then Grandma sighs.

'From the top of the stairs to the bottom. It's a wonder she didn't break her neck.'

Then Grandad says something with such bitterness it makes Kezia gasp and her insides curdle. 'I'd like to break *his* neck.'

'Me too.' This from Grandma is even more shocking. Kezia keeps very still so Rosie doesn't notice. Another transgression on this bizarre evening. It's as if the presenter of *Final Score* has thrown away the rule book and is shouting the football scores at the top of his voice.

She can hear them both slurp their tea. And then Grandma clears her throat and makes a sound as if she's getting up again. 'Well, we'll tell Roy's son about it. Make sure he knows it still hurts her.'

Then she walks into the parlour, leaving Grandad at the table. Kezia sits up and turns her gaze to the television. She hopes Grandma doesn't notice anything, but can't see how she won't – it feels as if her heart has been rolled out, like a bread poultice, and painted over her body.

Grandma strokes Rosie's cheek and touches Kezia's

shoulder. She sits down.

Then Rosie says, 'Who do you think is more handsome, Grandma? Luke Duke or Bo Duke?'

The Ferrets

Kezia and Rosie are in the garden. They are at the bottom of the garden, near the fence separating Grandad's plot from the neighbour at the back, for they are making a fairy picnic with one of Grandma's roses, and it is vitally important that Grandma doesn't see. She doesn't grow them on purpose or know what they need to thrive, but they are very precious. If she catches Kezia and Rosie using one of the delicate pink heads as fairy food, she'd make that tight face of hers and suck her teeth.

The girls have made themselves a little den beside a rhododendron bush, out of sight of the kitchen window and have set out plates of leaves. Kezia tears rose petals into tiny pieces, a small line of sorrow threading through the movement of her fingers at the destruction of something so fragrant and beautiful, and places morsels on the leaves. She is reminded of Mrs Hartley's rose, pulled apart earlier in the summer, and feels a thrill of guilt all over again.

Rosie is holding her breath with the magic of it all. She lives in hope that fairies will one day descend on the picnic they've set out.

The last plate has almost been filled when a snuffling, brown face pokes through the bush. Rosie stares at it for a moment, non-believing, and then starts to shriek.

'A ferret! A ferret!'

Another face, this one patchy and grey, and then the

ferrets are out and among the fairy picnic. They scrabble about, darting between the girls. Kezia pulls her legs up and starts to holler. She's held one of Ferret Jack's pets before, but Rosie's terror is infectious.

'Grandad! Jack's ferrets are in the garden!'

Grandad pokes his head out of his shed, knocking aside old pram wheels cluttering the doorway. He's spent the morning repairing something. He looks down the garden crossly. 'What's that bloody noise?!'

'Grandad!' Rosie flies up the garden path towards him. Another ferret jumps in front of her, holding something brown and flapping in its jaw, and she stops abruptly. She turns her face to the sky. Kezia cringes, knowing what is coming.

Rosie's screams are the kind that make your teeth hurt, and Grandad drops the chisel he's holding and sprints to her. The kitchen door is flung open and Grandma is there. She's still holding the potato peeler.

'Rosie, oh my lord, is it your arm?' She reaches Rosie before Grandad does, moving shockingly fast for a plump woman. And then she sees the ferret and screams herself.

Kezia has turned herself into a stone and is still at the bottom of the garden. The ferrets have had a sniff of her shoes and lost interest. They've rushed back into the bushes.

'Bernard!' Grandma yelps. 'Fetch Jack!'

'I think he can hear us, woman,' Grandad snaps. 'The whole bloody street can hear us! Rosie, stop screaming.'

Rosie shuts her mouth with a snap and whimpers to be

picked up. She's quite tall for five and heavier than she was at the start of the summer, so Grandad struggles to lift her. But he manages it, groaning as he swings her onto his hip.

'Kezia!' he yells, despite his grumble just a second ago about the noise they were all making. 'Make sure my greenhouse door is shut. If those things get in there and destroy my tomatoes, I'm going to shoot them!'

'You don't have a gun, Bernard, don't be so dramatic.' Irony isn't one of Grandma's strong points and she doesn't notice Grandad's eyebrows shoot up. 'Kezia!" she says sternly. "Come up here at once. Inside, girls, get inside. Oh, lord, I've left the back door open.'

They bustle to the kitchen door and Grandad kicks aside Rosie's dolls pram in the hurry to get inside. Then they are all in and Grandad shuts the door with a bang. They crowd the kitchen window to watch the ferrets, now numbering five, snout around the garden.

'What's Jack's telephone number?' Grandma asks. 'You'd better phone him.'

'Why would I know his number?' Grandad splutters. 'He lives ten yards away!'

'Don't go out there, Grandad,' Rosie begs. She's sitting on the draining board where Grandad has deposited her. It's quite high up and her face is pink. Kezia can see the height has made her feel a little grand. 'They might bite your legs.'

'I'll stamp on the buggers,' Grandad grumbles.

Kezia giggles. She can't help herself.

'We have to tell Jack,' Grandma moans. 'We're trapped in

here until he catches them all. Trapped!'

'It's not Coldtiz, love,' but Grandad is thinking. The hair around his ears sticks out. There is a fleck of blue paint on his cheek and Kezia wonders for the first time what he was up to in his shed, and if Grandma would approve. 'There's only one thing for it," he says. "Where's my wellies, Edith?'

They find Grandad's wellies in the cupboard under the stairs, where they've sat since he last wore them in March, when the allotment was a sea of mud. There's still clots of earth on the soles, and Grandma tuts as he brings them into the kitchen. 'You couldn't have cleaned them, Bernard?'

'I'm a working man,' Grandad says, with authority. 'This is a sign of my labour.'

Grandma rolls her eyes but says nothing as he sits down and forces them onto his feet.

'Won't the ferrets jump into them?' Kezia asks. She shudders. The image of a scrabbling, biting warm bundle of fur trapped beside her skin makes her guts feel loose.

It strikes Grandad as awful, too, for he stands up and rummages around in the kitchen drawer under the sink. Rosie pulls her knees up to make space for him and watches, curiously.

Grandad reappears with a roll of parcel tape. 'Knew I had some left. Smart thinking, Kezia. Get me the scissors.'

Grandad tapes the wellies to his trousers, using reams of the roll, and when he stands up again, he looks like a baby penguin. They'd watched a documentary the other night after tea, about penguins in the snow, and the girls had laughed enough to cry at the sight of baby emperor penguins tottering unevenly on the ice. Even Grandma held a hand to her mouth to hide her smile.

Then Grandad opened the back door again with a flourish. 'I'm off! I may be some time!'

Kezia runs to the parlour window to watch him walk up the path to the front gate and out, and then into Jack's front garden next door. His bald pink head bobs behind the bushes. She returns to the kitchen, giggling softly.

'Will he be long, Grandma?' Rosie asks. She moves on the draining board, uncomfortable now.

'He better not,' Grandma says quietly. 'Kezia, grab that chair, will you, so Rosie can climb down.'

And then, just as Rosie is unpeeling her thighs from the draining board and stepping onto the chair, the telephone rings in the hallway. Grandma freezes. She's got a hand under Rosie's armpit, helping her down. A thought clouds her face.

'Oh, will this day never end? I'd forgotten Andy said he was going to call today.'

'Andy?' Rosie squeaks and climbs down in a hurry.

'Get a move on,' Grandma clucks. 'It's night time in Australia.'

'Night time?' Rosie stands on the kitchen carpet in her sandals. In all the excitement she has forgotten to take them off. Another transgression on this morning of strangeness. Rosie scowls. 'How can it be night time?'

'Because Australia is on the other side of the world,

dumbo.' Kezia rolls her eyes.

Grandma gives her a poke. 'One of you get the phone!'

Rosie throws Kezia a glare, as angry as she can make it, and pushes past. She clatters down the hall and they hear her squeal a hello into the phone. Andy, a mythical figure. Kezia can barely remember his face. When she thinks of him, she sees the photo taken at the airport just before he left. He's standing with his ticket in his hand, flanked by Grandad and Grandma. He's taller than Grandad and looks like both his parents, as if he was made of pieces of them and rolled together like salt dough, into his own colour.

The photo is five years old and was probably taken by Mum. She'd gone to the airport as well. Kezia imagines her balancing her elbows on her belly, filled with Rosie, as she pressed the button on the camera. It is a photo she sees every day but has faded a bit in the sun. Maybe it has leaked its brightness into Andy himself, who is apparently tanned like an old apple now. The only thing she can remember of him is a large freckle next to his nose and the bite of aftershave. There was something else, whispers between the adults about restricted movements, time spent in a place he didn't want to be – something had driven him to the tourist agent and airport. But Kezia has given up trying to find out more. The world of adults is a maze to her, a lattice of things that can and cannot be said.

Then Rosie is hollering. 'Kezia! He wants to talk to you!'

Kezia shakes her head, wanting to leave Andy in the storybook she has put him in, but Grandma gives her a little push. 'Go on,' she hisses. 'One minute, that's all. I dread to think how much this call is costing him.'

When Kezia takes the phone from her sister, the creature on the other end is chuckling. Something Rosie has said has obviously amused him.

'Ferret Jack's lost his ferrets, then?' he says. He says 'Jack' oddly, stretching the word way longer than it needs. He laughs in a way Kezia hasn't heard before. She imagines him throwing his head back and opening his body to it. Grandad doesn't laugh like that. Dad doesn't. They titter, as if skating on the edges of whatever they find funny, frightened to dive in.

'Grandad's gone next door to tell him,' she says.

'Can't remember how many times that happened when I was a kid. You mum was shit-scared of them. Oh, sorry.'

Kezia grins.

'Been there all summer, kid?' There's a noise in the background, on the farm in some dusty patch of earth. A clanging noise as Andy moves the handset to his other ear. 'Bored yet?'

'It's all right. We have a lot of stews.'

'Rabbit? Sounds about right.' *Abbaaat.* He laughs again. 'Your Grandad says he doesn't like them at the allotment, but he doesn't mind them in the pot. You speak to Anna much?'

It's like she has to translate him. *He means Mum.* Kezia glances over her shoulder, to the kitchen where Grandma is leaning over Rosie's knee, examining a scrape. It's good she is distracted. She senses Andy doesn't care much for rules. He might tell her something.

'A bit. She's in Germany.'

'With the new fella?' Andy scoffs. 'Well, he's not exactly new. Surprised she didn't end up with him the first time around. Don't worry about it, kid. Grown-ups fuck up from time to time. Sorry. But we do. Not usually as bad as your Dad and me, when I was younger... perhaps I shouldn't say that.'

Kezia feels dizzy. His words spin beneath her feet and she can't catch herself. She hears a kitchen cupboard open and a tin being rattled and knows, without looking round that Grandma is finding a plaster to put on Rosie's knee. Everything has a place in the kitchen. 'Who is he?'

'Old friend,' Andy says flatly. 'Don't tell your Grandma I've told you anything. Some things they don't want mentioned, you know. Anyway, he's got a good job. Army bloke now, stationed in Germany. Signed up when your mum and Dad got together but kept in touch. Ah, well. Let's hope he makes better decisions than your Dad did. Want to know how many calves I delivered today?'

'What's delivered?' Kezia asks faintly. Her insides feel shivery. What's a fella?

'Oh, you've not learned about in school yet? Delivered means having a kid, kid. Ha! Seven calves today. Seven! I'll send you a photo. Right, stick your Grandma on, there's a love. Be good, Kez.'

Kezia whispers goodbye and rests the phone carefully

down on the table. She walks unsteadily back into the kitchen. Grandma is washing her hands and looks up.

'My turn?' she says brightly. 'Won't be long.' She disappears into the hallway and they hear her laughing, immediately, into the phone.

Rosie looks at her sister suspiciously. Kezia is wobbly and sits down on a chair. She feels sick.

'What's wrong?' Rosie says. 'You look like you're going to barf.'

Kezia shakes her head. She can't weave her thoughts properly together. *Fella* means man. Boyfriend. Mum has a boyfriend? What about Dad?

'Are you thinking about the ferrets?' Rosie shudders. 'I hate their teeth. One of them had caught a bird, Kezia. A *bird*. Disgusting.'

'Cats catch birds,' Kezia says. She swallows hard.

'But that's normal. That's what cats are supposed to do.'

'Maybe ferrets are supposed to as well.'

'I don't think so,' Rosie scoffs.

'Jack says they are good for catching rats.'

'That's different. What are dogs supposed to do, Kez?'

Both girls look at Missy, asleep as usual in front of the gas fire. The old dog is on her side so they can see her faded brown teats.

'I don't know,' Kezia says. She feels like she's recovering slightly. 'Keep you company?'

Rosie gives a little toss of her head. 'That's not right. Mum would have kept her and Missy would have lived with us, if that was true. Maybe the farts put her off.'

Kezia giggles. It's true. Missy is a terrible farter. 'She's worse than Grandad.'

Rosie lifts up her bum and pretends to blast off. 'Remember that one she did last night after tea? Egg!'

The girls lean together, conspiratorially, chuckling. Missy had disgraced herself the night before. Grandma was going to put her outside until Grandad resisted.

'Dad was worse, though,' Rosie muses. Then she stops giggling and looks down. She's barely mentioned their father all summer. 'I wonder where he is.'

He's now the old fella, Kezia thinks, but says nothing. Andy's words ring in her ears. Dad had *fucked up*. She lets the phrase widen in her mind, letters rising gloriously. She knows if she says them out loud she would be in real trouble. Might even get her bottom spanked. They are untethered words, so shocking and raw and impressive.

Her brain feels as if it might spill from her ears and she feels suddenly very tired. She wants Grandad to come back and be daft, and for them to play Snakes and Ladders, going up the ladders and sliding down the snakes in the way they're supposed to. She won't even cheat if they could just have a game and forget about the ferrets and Andy's call.

Then, as if he has heard her, Grandad appears in the garden. He's with Jack, a thin old man with greasy hair and a pipe clenched between his teeth. They are both holding big sticks.

'What are they doing?' Kezia gets up and goes to the sink.

Rosie pulls the chair over and climbs up to see as well.

They see that the men aren't holding sticks after all, but nets. Huge ones, big enough to catch a whale. They start running round the garden, sweeping them high and low, shouting to each other.

'They're trying to catch the ferrets!' Rosie squeals. She clambers onto the draining board. 'Look!'

The girls stare, and stare more at the spectacle and then, as Jack stands up triumphantly with a squirming ball of fur in his net, they start to laugh.

The Birthday

It's Kezia's birthday. She wakes early to the smell of frying mushrooms and lies in bed, trying to remember where she is. Rosie is at the other end, hugging Kezia's legs. For once Kezia doesn't kick her away. It's early enough to not be too hot and Grandma let them keep the window open overnight, so the bedroom feels cool.

The blankets are scrunched up on the floor, save for one thin sheet covering both girls. Grandma doesn't do duvets. When they first came to stay, Kezia couldn't get used to going to sleep under scratchy orange blankets, and tossed and turned until Grandma took a bedsheet and sewed it to the blanket. The sheet has been washed so many times that it now feels soft as old skin.

She wonders what they will use if they are still living with Grandma and Grandad when the sun begins to fall from the sky in the middle of the afternoon and frost will bloom over Grandma's roses. Maybe Grandma will relent and send Grandad to buy duvets from the linen store on the market. Kezia doesn't know how she feels about the idea.

She can hear Grandad humming downstairs. It's Sunday, the one morning when Grandma tries to sleep in, and the old man is up making breakfast. She imagines him flicking mushrooms over in the pan, adding salt from the pot with the clipper painted on the side. Kezia's tried to draw the ship and has almost managed it perfectly. She wriggles happily.

There'll be bacon as well, going on soon, as a birthday treat.

Finally she slips her legs from Rosie's grasp, who mumbles and turns over, but doesn't wake. It's warm enough not to need a dressing gown, so Kezia potters down the stairs in her pyjamas. Through Grandma's open bedroom door, she can see a shape rising and falling rhythmically. A soft snore.

Grandad grins when she comes into the kitchen. He's wearing one of Grandma's tabards – not the weekend one, but another that was probably due for the wash – and he holds up a spatula dramatically.

'She appears!' he says in a loud whisper. 'The birthday girl.'

Kezia smiles dopily and slides onto a chair. Grandad looks ridiculous. Missy ambles in from the parlour and nudges her knee. She receives the obligatory morning pat on the top of her head and goes to lie by the fire. There is a groove in the rug where her heavy body lies, day after day.

'I was going to bring you breakfast in bed!' Grandad says. He takes a slurp of his tea. 'Want mushrooms?'

Kezia considers. 'How have you cut them?'

Grandad takes the frying pan off the stove and shows her. He's cut the big button mushrooms in half and left the small ones intact.

Kezia smiles in approval. She can't stand mushrooms that have been sliced into thin strips. They remind her of worms. 'Yes please.'

'We'll give everyone another five minutes and we'll shout

for them to come down.' Grandad spoons another pat of lard into the pan. 'Dripping on toast?'

This is the best part of a weekend breakfast. When they first came to stay, the sight of creamy fat streaked with brown in the dripping pot made Kezia feel sick. It looked like earwax. Rosie point-blank refused to touch it. But even Grandma eats it on toast, so Kezia tried it. She found she liked the coffee-coloured blobs most of all, for they tasted of meat. Grandad puts a plate of toast in front of her and she takes the earthenware pot and smears dripping on top.

He watches and nods. 'Good lass. That'll put hairs on your chest.'

Another of his sayings, she's heard it before. She's supposed to say in return – 'but I'm a girl' – and, because it's her birthday and she doesn't feel sad, Kezia does. Then a thought occurs and the words are out before she can stop them.

'Did my mum like beef dripping when she was little?'

Grandad pauses over the frying pan. A frown on his face, which he tries to hide. The toast is a brick in Kezia's mouth. The feeling of heaviness which has clung to her for days, except for this most precious of mornings, slams back into her.

'Not really,' Grandad says eventually. 'Your Uncle Andy did.'

'What about mushrooms?' Kezia can't believe she's asking more. But, as it's her birthday, she wonders if Grandad will open up and tell her something about her mother. It's bright and early and sun streams through the kitchen window, turning the bottle of washing-up liquid into a collection of emeralds, and the clock ticks round like a steady companion. Kezia can see lint and dust in the air; it seems as if the house has momentarily slipped free of its mooring on Vernon Street, free of its place in the row of pre-war semi-detached houses with identical front lawns and paths and on the 318 bus route into town. At this very moment while Rosie and Grandma sleep upstairs, 3 Vernon Street is a floating space where anything might happen or be said.

Grandad sighs and turns off the gas under the frying pan. He sits down opposite Kezia. He places a thick hand against the silver teapot and pours himself a fresh mug.

'This has been an upside down few weeks for you girls, hasn't it?' he says. 'I don't think you're really interested in whether your mum liked dripping or mushrooms.'

Kezia shakes her head. She can't look at him.

'It's all right to be curious,' Grandad says. 'But there are things that can't be said around Rosie. You do understand that?'

Kezia gives the tiniest nod.

'Okay then. What do you want to know? Ask me.'

Kezia swallows the toast, forcing it down. Now Grandad has opened up like a book, she doesn't know which bit to read first. It's like the collection of fairy stories she was given for her birthday last year – so many, the contents list ran for three pages. She wanted to read them all, to take them in in one gulp, and it overwhelmed her. She'd burst into tears.

She's older now and doesn't cry. But she still doesn't know what to ask and finally looks up at Grandad helplessly.

He seems to understand. He pats her hand. 'What happened at Christmas to Rosie shouldn't have happened. At all. Now, I know your mum said it was an accident, and of course that's what your dad said too. But nothing like that ever happened in *this* house, and your Grandma and I certainly had our share of arguments.'

He's started with the worst of it. That awful, awful Christmas. Rosie at the top of the stairs, holding onto Mum's dress. Kezia at the bottom, colouring book in her hand, craning her neck to see what was going on, only hearing words that she didn't understand and Dad angrier than ever. A movement, Mum stumbling backwards, and Rosie flying down the stairs, rolling as if she was a gymnast. But, of course, she wasn't Olga Korbut, and she landed at the bottom in a pile that didn't look right. Her arm twisted in an ugly way. Screaming.

It wasn't like the time Kezia jumped from the top of the stairs, just to see if she could. Rosie hadn't wanted to fly through the air. She hadn't planned it when she'd clung to Mum, turning her tear-streaked face up to her Dad, who was yelling and waving his arms around.

Kezia wipes her eyes with the heel of her hand. She thinks Grandad will stop talking – he hates to see her crying – but this is a magical morning and the kitchen is a little bubble where the usual rules don't apply. He rubs his own face and touches her arm again, and sits up ready for questions.

'Do you think he'll come back?' Kezia whispers.

'You'll see him again, for sure,' Grandad says. He leans forward. 'But this next bit is very important. We have to make sure you and Rosie are safe. Do you understand?'

'Safe.'

'Yes. Safe as houses. Your mum – well, she never quite managed it.' A hard look on Grandad's face, one Kezia has never seen before. She wonders if Grandad is madder at Mum than Dad for what happened to Rosie.

'Is that why she's in Germany?' Kezia asks. 'To find somewhere Rosie and I can be kept safe?'

Grandad picks up his mug of tea and covers his mouth. 'That's what she thinks she's doing, yes. How would you feel about that?'

'Going to Germany?' Kezia is shocked. The possibility hasn't crossed her mind.

'It's not my place to say why she's there and your mum will tell you when the time is right. But you and Rosie might not have to go. Your Grandma and I have been speaking to Roy's son. There might be another way.' And then Grandad is done. The shape of his shoulders tells Kezia he won't say anymore. She wants him to carry on but also doesn't want him to – the freedom to ask and be told anything is terrifying for a little girl. Part of her wants Grandad to tell her about Roy's son and what he's really doing for Grandma and Grandad, and why that means they don't have enough money to go on holiday this summer. But part of her doesn't. The Kezia who is afraid of the dark, and snuggles against Grandma's side when they watch telly at night and see Basil Rathbone chase a hound across the moors, doesn't want to hear anymore. Basil is braver than her.

Kezia grips her plate. She watches Grandad tip his tea down his throat in a single torrent and wipe his lips.

'Right, I think that's enough for now,' he says. 'Finish up that toast and then go and wake your Grandma. We have bacon to eat!'

Forced, thin joviality. But an adult's way of making the best of things and covering up, and Kezia is used to it. She eats her toast as Grandad gets up and turns back to the cooker. She sees him frown at the grill that juts out over the four gas rings, calculating if he should cook the bacon on there or fry it. Please fry it, she thinks. It's my birthday.

Then Grandad winks at her and tips the mushrooms into the glass bowl usually used for allotment salad, and scoops a dollop of dripping from the earthenware pot into the frying pan. The bacon is wrapped in greaseproof paper – good, thick bacon from Ernest the Butcher in town. Kezia smiles, almost happy again, and watches Grandad lay the slices in the pan.

She finishes the last of her toast and trots upstairs to wake up Grandma. Grandma is already sitting up in bed. She stretches out her arms when Kezia walks in, doughy arms extending from a cream-coloured nightie.

'My big girl!' she says. 'Come here!'

They hug. Grandma smells warm and soapy and Kezia

lies half across her. There are an impossible number of pillows propping Grandma up. Kezia can't understand how she can sleep with so many pillows on the bed and wonders if she puts them somewhere when it's time to sleep. But she's never seen the pillows on the floor, only on the bed.

Kezia sits up. 'Grandad's cooking birthday bacon.'

'The smell woke me up. Lovely. I can't believe you're eight, Kezia.' Grandma leans forward and catches Kezia's face in her hands. 'I remember how tiny you were. Three weeks early. You were like a little mouse.'

It's a story Kezia has heard hundreds of times before – she had been underweight and none of the clothes her mum had packed to go to the hospital fit. So Grandad went to Mrs Lacey's Clothing Emporium on the high street and paid an obscene amount of money for premature baby-grows and booties, all for his first grandchild. After he'd first held Kezia and had a little sob over her fingers and toes, he'd sat in the waiting room and sweated over how much money he'd spent.

Usually the story of Grandad rushing out to buy expensive baby clothes is remembered at times when he's done something else daft – like when he'd grabbed Rosie's Barbie doll to swot a wasp in the window or, somehow, shut the piano lid on his own fingers. But, this morning, when Kezia thinks of Grandad holding a miniature set of baby clothes, her throat feels tight and her nose prickles.

Grandma cocks her head to the side. 'You all right, darling? Your mum will call today, you'll see.'

Kezia shakes her head. 'It's nothing.'

Rosie appears in the doorway, holding a Barbie doll by the hair, blinking away the last dregs of sleep. 'What's Grandad doing?'

When they get downstairs, Grandad has laid the table and filled their favourite mugs with tea or squash. Grandma has her rose tea cup and saucer, Grandad his mug of see-through, tempered glass. The blue mug for Kezia, showing Jerry whacking Tom with a mallet, and the brown one for Rosie where Jerry is sitting in an egg cup. Grandad waves his arms over the table dramatically. Each plate has a pile of mushrooms, two slices of bacon and, on his own and Grandma's plate, he's added a fried tomato from his allotment.

'Bernard,' Grandma says in a soft voice, and touches him on the shoulder.

The bacon is too thick and tough for Rosie to cut up, so Grandma lets her use her fingers to eat it, just this one time. She chews noisily but Kezia doesn't mind, on this upside-down morning. Tears feel close by and she tries not to move her head too quickly in case they shake free. She stares at her Tom and Jerry mug, filled as it always is, with orange squash. Small points of order and steadiness, and Kezia casts about for them.

It is not long before they finish and Grandad scrapes the last bits of bacon fat left on Rosie's plate into Missy's dog bowl. Another cup of tea. Grandma gets up while Grandad is filling her cup and goes into the parlour.

She appears with two presents. They are wrapped in red and gold tissue paper, and tied together with a shiny, scarlet ribbon. Kezia sees the ribbon before anything else. Its luxuriousness delights her. She imagines it sewn onto the trim of her latest gypsy caravan, made with the tube from a ream of kitchen roll.

Grandma sits down again and hands the presents to Kezia. 'Happy birthday. It's not much but I hope you like them.'

Rosie pulls a face, annoyed at the fuss, but cranes to see what the presents are. The first one, on the top, is easy – even she can tell it's a book. Kezia unwraps it carefully, trying not to rip the delicate tissue paper. She has plans for that as well.

It's a book of Sherlock Holmes stories. Rosie sighs, disappointed, but a new book is fine by Kezia. She flips through it, seeing herself later that day, reading it while sprawled on the settee while Grandad watches the Grand Prix.

'What's in the big one, Kezia?' Rosie urges.

The bigger present is soft and squashy and, for a wild moment, Kezia wonders if it's what she'd hoped for and not dared to say. In the window of Mrs Lacey's Clothing Emporium are cushions. Not just any old cushions, or like the ones Grandma makes, but ones covered in red and green sequins. They shimmer as the sun moves around the glass. They peacock and entice and Kezia adores them. They are like jewels on the high street, with a price-tag to match.

But, of course, it's not a cushion. Instead it's a jumper, knitted by Grandma. Kezia sighs a little – she should have known. She and Rosie always get a knitted jumper on their birthdays. They usually go baggy after being put in the wash, and one time Grandma made Kezia a jumper with the most horrendous, fluffy white wool that moulted like Missy sometimes does. Fluff would find her way into Kezia's mouth and throat whenever she wore it. She hated it.

But this new jumper is stripy, in blue and red and yellow and green, so it's bright and cheerful and Kezia doesn't think she will mind wearing it. She wonders when Grandma knitted it. It must have been in the evenings, when they had gone to bed. The thought that Grandma has kept such a secret and done it just for Kezia makes her feel a little dizzy.

'It's very pretty,' Rosie says. She reaches out to touch it, fingers smeary with grease and Kezia edges away.

'No, Rosie.' Kezia feels a little superior. 'You'll get it dirty.'

'That's a sign to get the washing-up done,' Grandad says. He gets up and starts shuffling plates together, stacking them up. 'Rosie, my gal, you can help me. Pull your chair over to the sink and stand on it – you can do the washing.'

An unexpected treat, and Rosie doesn't mind at all. The steel sink is deep and takes ages to fill with water – the girls have both had baths in it when they were little – and Rosie leans her little body into it as the water pours. She giggles as Grandad puts an extra-large squirt of washing-up liquid in, and shakes her hands to make bubbles.

'Why don't you go upstairs and get dressed?' Grandma says, leaning next to Kezia and pressing her mouth to the top of her head. 'Let me see you in your new jumper?'

Kezia smiles and nods. It's going to be a good day, after all. She pushes away the memory of stairs and her sister's twisted body lying at her feet. The kitchen lights up with morning sun and foam floats from the sink on the air. Rosie is laughing and Grandad is splashing her. Kezia holds her rainbow jumper, knitted by Grandma, hugging it tightly to her body, and then slips from her chair and goes upstairs.

The Library

The girls are at the library. It's a jewel of a place and when Grandma got them to put their shoes on and told them where they were going, Kezia thought all the air in her throat would boil and leave her body in one excited rush. The library sits in the middle of the town precinct, opposite Fine Fare where Grandad buys his tins and washing power, and it's the most graffitied building in the place. Bright blue paint is splashed over every wall - 'Jake loves Michelle', 'Callum is a fanny' – and usually Grandma rushes the girls past to the library front door so they can't see every word. But it's a place Kezia dreams about and holds the memory of in her nose – old paper, floor polish, coffee. The books she takes back to Grandma's house keep a deposit of the library's scent in their spines and covers. They are islands, links on a daisy chain.

The shops surrounding the library face all sides of the building. The library is built over two floors and wide glass windows line the whole of the second floor. Glass is turned into mirrors as the sun moves around the precinct. Grandad once told the girls about a seagull who stood too long in the library's reflected glare and spontaneously combusted. Rosie believed him.

Even the graffiti seems, to Kezia, perfectly placed. She always cranes her neck around Grandma's rump to see the words. The painted insults and scowling cartoon faces are fissures. She spies the land of adult through them. She doesn't know what every word means and would rather die than ask, but they are shouty markers of a world both terrifying and enticing.

Rosie likes the library front door best of all. Or, specifically, the door handle. It's huge, shaped like a tea tray, and has a bobbled surface that is smooth to touch. It's like a bundle of balloons underwater or a bag of emeralds at the bottom of a lake. She lingers at the front door every time they visit the library and tries to run her fingertips over every raised surface. It's sea-green in colour and one of Rosie's deepest wishes is to find a felt-tip in the same hue. Kezia thinks Rosie might wet herself if she actually finds one.

Today is a spinning plate. They are at the library but Grandma and Grandad have left them in the care of Miss Sybil, the librarian who smells of talcum powder and something fecund and rather disgusting. And they haven't been left at the Children's Section. Grandma and Grandad have rushed the girls in, hauling Rosie past the door handle, depositing them at the lending desk with a paper bag of boiled sweets and a stern reminder to be good. It's obvious this arrangement has been made in advance, for Miss Sybil nods and stands up when they arrive at the desk.

'We'll be an hour,' Grandma says, more to Miss Sybil than the girls and, without even dropping a kiss on the tops of their heads, pulls her coat around her and bustles away. Kezia's mouth falls open. This has never happened before.

'Where are you going?' she asks. She holds her pile of

books, ready to exchange, and her hands start to sweat.

'Be good, girls,' Grandad says, and even he is distracted. He slips a ten pence coin into Kezia's cardigan pocket. 'If you get thirsty, pour yourself a cup of squash from the jug. Remember to pay for it.'

The plate wobbles. Another first. They never get a drink at the library. Grandma doesn't even buy a cup of tea while waiting for the girls to choose their books for machine tea tastes – Grandad says – of cat's piss.

Miss Sybil smiles and nods and comes around the desk to stand with the girls as Grandma and Grandad hurry out. Grandma is tying her headscarf on and Kezia sees her fingers fumble with the knot under her chin. Another strange thing – Grandma can usually tie that thing with one hand. But not today. Kezia watches them walk back up the precinct and round a corner. They disappear.

Rosie's eyes are wet. She's blinking fiercely and slides closer to Kezia. Miss Sybil cocks her head towards her. Kezia is reminded of a toy dog Rosie once owned, with a fat wobbly head. Rosie used to shake, shake, shake it, until one day the head really did bounce off and left an ugly rusting spring.

'Don't worry, girls. It will just be for an hour,' Miss Sybil says. There's a mole on her chin. 'And there's plenty to entertain you here! Rosie, we have new colouring sheets on the table in the children's section. Want to see?'

The woman's voice has a weird pitch to it and Kezia has learned enough this summer to tell when an adult doesn't mean what they are saying. She knows Miss Sybil, of course – all the children do. She stamps their books and reminds them when a loan is overdue. She's nice. But today she sounds odd.

Rosie hasn't noticed. She wants to go through to the children's section, to the colouring sheets. Her little body twitches and Kezia can see she's conflicted. 'Will you come with me, Kez?' she asks quietly. Rosie's developed a hard lump on the middle finger of her right hand from all the colouring she's done and her tight grip of the felt-tips – it's a source of pride for her this summer. The walls of their bedroom at Grandma's are dotted with bright pictures of castles and Fergie's honeymoon clothes.

'I'll take you,' Miss Sybil says. 'I expect Kezia might want to look at the general fiction section.'

Kezia catches her breath. She thinks she might have misheard. The general fiction section is where the adult books are. Books with black covers and wolves with red fangs, and grey-faced men in hats smoking thin cigarettes. Grandma hasn't let her borrow books from that section.

'Yes, please,' she mumbles. She prays Rosie won't say anything or insist she is only allowed to borrow from the children's shelves. But Rosie has slipped her hand into Miss Sybil's and seems to have recovered. Just to be sure, Kezia gives her sister the bag of boiled sweets. 'You take them,' she says. 'Save me some.'

This unusual morning is becoming a very good morning for Rosie and she finally grins, showing the goofy gap in her teeth. She wanders away with Miss Sybil. Kezia hears her sandals slap on the linoleum floor and then the sound is muffled by the carpet in the children's section. The carpet is bright red, clashing violently with the blue plastic floor throughout the rest of the library. The children's section is a little island of colour, set apart from the rest of the building.

Whistling casually, Kezia leaves the books she's returning on the desk and clasps her hands behind her back. She glides over to the nearest shelf of books. She keeps her movements as smooth as the conveyor belt on *The Generation Game* they watch on Saturday nights. A prize one week had even been a set of encyclopaedias.

Kezia stands in front of the books. She can't believe she's doing this. The rows of titles threaten to overwhelm her. Her eyes scan the shelves erratically and her throat itches. Just how does a grown-up choose what to read!

Then she sees that the books on the shelves are ordered alphabetically by author and she sighs in relief. A little foothold, an order she can understand. She hears Rosie's laugh and the sound of a chair banging. Her sister will be sitting down at the children's table, reaching for a colouring pencil. The end will have been chewed by another child but Rosie will add her own teeth marks. Kezia hates it when she does this. Picking up a wet felt-tip at Grandma's house makes her stomach roil.

She's standing in front of the *G* section. *Gaskell, Gilman, Godwin...* Kezia breathes deeply and reaches for a book. It's by someone called Patricia Gout. Grandad says he has gout. It is something to do with his feet. The front cover isn't of feet, though, but of a cottage and a woman in a fancy old dress looking sad. Kezia puts it back. She doesn't know exactly what she's looking for but the films she watched at the start of the summer don't appeal to her now. Love affairs are boring. Feeling braver, she looks elsewhere, at other books on the shelves.

The books are smaller than the ones in the children's section and the print is tiny, but that doesn't scare Kezia. She's already read the Sherlock Holmes book Grandma and Grandad gave her for her birthday. Her favourite story in there is the one about the orange pips. She's read it over and over. The best way to read it was under a blanket with Grandad's torch when they thought she was getting in her pyjamas after her bath.

She stands in front of the shelf marked *H* and then sees them. A line of books by the same author. Black covers, red and white lettering on the spines. Someone called James Herbert. Kezia takes one down and holds it in her hands. The sounds of the library float away. She can no longer hear the chatter from the children's section or the sound of the drinks machine churning out tepid brown water, or the assistant librarian stamping someone's card. She stares down. A huge rat with blood dripping from its whiskers glares back up at her.

This. This is the book she wants to read. It lies in her hands like a hot ember. The title is made up of jagged letters and she thinks of the graffiti on the side of the library. The spine seems to crack and, as the library door opens, the cover flutters open. Kezia glimpses words, a typed path spiralling away.

'That's a good book.'

Kezia jumps. Somehow Miss Sybil has drifted from Rosie's colouring table and stands beside her. Kezia closes the book and glances up. For the first time she notices that from under Miss Sybil's left sleeve, a green snake's head slithers down her arm. Kezia gapes. A tattoo.

'Might be a bit scary for you, though.' Miss Sybil reaches up to touch the shelf and the snake on her arm fully appears. Its tongue is forked and bright red. Kezia watches it. Can women have tattoos?

'He did a series,' and Miss Sybil traces her fingers over the spines. 'Yes, here's the second one. Also terrifying. What about this instead?''

She puts another book in Kezia's sweaty hands. This one has a girl in a raincoat standing in front of a ramshackle mansion, vines dripping from windows, a door hanging from its hinges. *The Haunting of Belleville Manor.*

'Your mum loved this,' Miss Sybil says. Again, her voice sounds wonky. She hesitates before she speaks, as if she's listening to the words in her head before saying them out loud. 'The scarier the better.'

'She did?' Kezia's thighs are weak, as if she has been swimming. She can't remember her mum reading a book. The covers of the book in her hands is bright and garish and nothing at all like the plain books Grandma has on her shelves. She's tried to read those but they don't make any sense. Characters speak to each other in words that seem to run across the whole page. She can't imagine her mum being a little girl and reading them.

'Sure. We used to sneak here after school and borrow them. She always took them out on my ticket.' Miss Sybil winks.

Kezia stares at her. She knows it's rude to stare but she can't help it. The woman can't be as old as she first thought. It's hard to judge. Miss Sybil wears sandals and ugly brown tights, but she has an earring on the top of her ear. And then there's that tattoo. The belt around her pinafore dress has a thin, almost invisible line of sequins.

'You were at school with my mum?'

Miss Sybil does that strange thing with her mouth again, as if she's holding words on her tongue, and then nods. 'We were a little gang. Three of us – your mum, me, and Joel. Good friends. You look like her.'

Joel? The name bounces in Kezia's skull, a firefly knocking against bone. 'Who's Joel?'

Miss Sybil holds her breath, as if she's standing on the edge of a pool, and then her words tumble out. 'Boy at school. Tall. Lived with his dad. Mum died. We looked out for him.'

'Mum's never talked about a Joel.'

Miss Sybil shrugs. 'She obviously didn't talk about me either. Joel joined the army around the same time as your mum got married.'

The army. Kezia feels words build up around her, blocks and scaffolds. She thinks she almost understands but then can't quite make out exactly what she thinks she knows. Words give answers and are windows but sometimes the glass is glazed.

'You were all friends?' she asks. It isn't quite the question she wants to ask, for she wants to know more about this Joel person, but the library floor feels unsteady beneath her jelly legs.

'Thick as thieves for a while.' Miss Sybil smiles like Grandad does when he's talking about the men he knew in the war. 'Spent most of our summers here. None of us wanted to be at home much." She looks over her shoulder, towards the Children's Section, but Rosie is still engrossed in colouring. "You won't know about the baby, before your Mum and Andy were born. Your Grandma used to get very sad about it. Being at the library became your mum's favourite thing."

"I didn't know," Kezia says. She wants to say she doesn't know any of it, but thinks that might stop Miss Sybil telling her anything.

"Hmm," Miss Sybil hums. "Then your dad came on the scene. Then you, of course. Your mum invited me to the wedding but I couldn't go.'

Kezia's head spins. She thinks of Grandma and the strange day of the storm. How Grandma had started to cry and that the day itself seemed to mean something.

'Your mum sent me a photo of her wedding day,' Miss Sybil is saying. 'Pretty dress.'

'It was white and very long.' Kezia remembers the photograph and she grabs onto it in her mind. It had been on top of the telly at home. At some point it disappeared. Mum was bigger in the photo than she is now. She had a little pot belly under the dress.

'Yes, well, I'm sure it was a nice day.' Miss Sybil clears her throat. 'Anyway, if you like horror, we've got the new Stephen King. Maybe for when you're older.'

'I've never heard of him.' Kezia suddenly feels very hot.

'Oh, dear, you're in for a treat.' Miss Sybil laughs and as she reaches to brush hair from her face, Kezia sees the faded half-moon under her armpit. 'Try the Belleville Manor first. Actually, there's something quite special about this book.'

'There is?'

'Each chapter ends where the reader has to decide what the heroine does next.' Miss Sybil takes the book from Kezia and flips through the pages. "See? At the end of this chapter you have to decide whether she goes down into the cellar to investigate the strange noises or goes up to the attic to look for the dead housekeeper's diary. Different pages for each choice. You get to decide the way the story will go.'

'I do?' Kezia's voice is a pearl of wonder. She's never heard anything like it.

'There are books in the children's section like this, but this one is much better. It's up to you, Kezia, where the heroine goes next. It's your choice.'

For a second she thinks Miss Sybil might be playing with her, but there the options are– stark on the page. *Go to page 28 if you choose the cellar. Go to page 36 if you choose the attic.* Kezia can't believe it. To have such power, such direction over a life, feels extraordinary.

'I don't think I want it,' she says, and steps back. She suddenly wants Grandma to return.

'Be brave, Kezia,' Miss Sybil says firmly and taps the book in Kezia's hands.

'Did my mum really like this book?' Kezia looks around the library, at the heavy bookcases and solid lending desk that had worn thick grooves into the carpet. Light streams through the windows and falls over her face. She squints uncomfortably but doesn't move. Lint floats on the air, microscopic diamonds turning in the sun.

'Devoured it. I wonder if she reads as much now.''

She doesn't say it as an admonishment, but Kezia feels guilty. Another layer of feeling painted on the day. Even in the weeks after Dad left and the girls started going to bed early, Mum still didn't read. If Kezia sneaked downstairs, Mum would be on the telephone to someone or staring at the telly. In the morning, she'd never remember what she'd watched.

'Maybe when she comes back, she can show you the books she used to borrow,' Miss Sybil says suddenly. That smell again, wafting from her. It's earthy and composty. The sides of her head, where hair grows up into her ponytail, are damp. 'Might be worth sorting out cards for you and your sister.'

'We've got library cards,' Kezia says. She points at the books she's left on the lending desk. 'See?'

Miss Sybil shakes her head. 'Not quite. That's something I've sorted out for your Grandma. But if you're - well, if you're going to be spending more time at your grandparents' house, you might as well have your own ticket so you can borrow whatever you want.'

Kezia frowns. Mum's due back next week and then she and Rosie are going home. Aren't they? She thinks of Grandad's red calendar from the newspaper, pinned to the kitchen wall, blocks of days marked out with a cross drawn in felt-tip. Mum's arrival back from Germany has been pencilled in. And then Kezia remembers another thing Grandad has written on the calendar, in the box above the date Mum will be back. *Stephen, office, 2pm.*

'Is it the eighteenth today?' she asks suddenly.

'The eighteenth? Yes, I think so.'

Kezia eyes feel heavy, as if there is a bubble of water about to break through and cascade down her face. She stares hard at the lettering on the book's front cover and tries not to cry.

Miss Sybil shifts her weight on her sandaled feet and hums. She's really sweating now. Kezia can't imagine her mum being friends with someone who sweats so much. She wonders again where Grandma and Grandad have gone.

'Why don't you take a seat and see if you like it?' Miss Sybil says and points to an empty chair in the corner of the library. She hasn't noticed the shake to Kezia's shoulders. 'I'll sit with Rosie. She's found a green felt-tip.'

The chair seems far away and Kezia doesn't feel like she's walking but suddenly she's sitting down. Her mouth feels watery. She sniffs hard. The chair is hard beneath her but that's okay. The book shelves seem to shimmer. She blinks again and again, trying to force shape back into the things she's seeing. Grandma and Grandad have gone to see Roy's son. She's now certain of it. That's who Stephen is. The adult world floats around her like a sea. She imagines building blocks of different colours rising and falling in the air, not quite taking shape but looming together in a pattern that's almost recognisable. She presses herself back into the rigid chair, curling her feet around the base and holding on.

From somewhere Miss Sybil produces a bottle of cherry pop and nestles it against Kezia's side before going back to the children's section. She still hasn't noticed Kezia's tears, but Kezia has fought hard to keep them in. The chair she's sitting in is in a space that's tucked away from everyone else, between the children's section and the precinct outside. Alec the fishman has set up a table outside his shop and, as the library door swings open and closed, Kezia can hear his harsh, ugly shout proclaiming bargains and prawns only just past their sell-by date.

The book has become slippery in her hands. Kezia holds it tightly. She can't decide whether to read it. She wonders what Grandma would make of it. Then she thinks of her mother, imagining a blazing, colourful version of the woman she knows, sneaking books home to Grandma's house to read in the bathroom at night. What direction did Mum choose for the heroine when she read the book, the book Kezia holds now? Carefully, timidly, Kezia opens the front over and begins to read.

The Visit

Grandma's gone through a lot of handkerchiefs today. Rosie thinks she has a cold and has started sewing again, stitching a big letter E onto a plain white piece of cloth. She's been working on it, now and again, since the start of the summer, and the stitches are horridly jagged and uneven. One night she managed to sew the handkerchief to her dressing gown, making Grandad laugh helplessly as she wailed. Even Grandma smiled as she cut the stitches with scissors. Rosie wants to finish the handkerchief today because...

She won't say it and Kezia doesn't want her to either. Tomorrow Mum will be back and she'll come and collect the girls and take them home, or maybe somewhere else. Their summer with Grandma and Grandad will be over. Seven more crosses have been added to the calendar.

Rosie doesn't say it because, as she whispered to Kezia at night in the single bed, she thinks she might stop it from happening if she says the words out loud. She wants Mum to come back with her whole being. She's a rigid little Egyptian mummy next to Kezia, her narrow face a stone. 'What if she doesn't come, Kez? I think I might die.'

Kezia doesn't know what to say and, in a sign of how much her insides are like a washing machine at the very thought of Mum returning, pats Rosie on the shoulder sympathetically. In the morning Grandma starts to go through handkerchiefs, nose and eyes leaking as she makes the girls' toast or peeling potatoes for lunch. Grandad spends more time banging and hammering in his shed.

When Mum phoned the other night, her voice had a laugh to it that Kezia hadn't heard in ages. She rang just as they were about to eat fish and chips. The week had been full of treats – chips, dripping on toast, cherry pop, black and white films on the telly whether snooker was on or not. Rosie had been so happy. The battered fish, though, had tasted like cardboard in Kezia's mouth and she had been relieved to escape to the phone when it rang. She couldn't look at Grandma, who had bowed her head over her plate and was chewing mechanically.

'Make sure you have all your things ready!' Mum had said breathlessly. 'I want to hear everything you've been up to this summer. And I have lots to tell you!'

Kezia had squeezed her eyes shut. The back door banged open and shut, for the day was hot and Grandad had threatened to sit at the kitchen table in his vest, and the sound made Kezia jump. She mumbled something. As she handed the phone over to Rosie, she heard an announcement over a tannoy in German.

It's after lunch and Grandad has disappeared into his shed again. He hasn't made one joke today. He's patted Kezia on the head several times and let Rosie brush his hair with her Barbie comb. He didn't clear the plates from the table and for once Grandma didn't tut.

Grandma's at the sink when Rosie slides into the kitchen.

Her face is pink. She's holding a small parcel wrapped in Christmas paper. Kezia sits with Missy on the rug in front of the gas fire. She knows what's in the present. She buries her nose in Missy's fur.

'I've finished it, Grandma,' Rosie says shyly. She sticks out her arms. The paper is slightly damp from her sweaty paws.

Grandma looks round, her brow frowned, and wipes her hands on the tea towel. 'What you got there, kiddo?'

Again, forced – kiddo is a word Grandma doesn't say. Kezia breathes in Missy's old smell. She's ready to run to the bathroom to fetch toilet roll for the tears. She gets up silently and fetches the roll as Grandma opens the parcel and sees the handkerchief, the letter *E* uneven but recognisable. Grandma pulls Rosie to her, crushing the girl against her tabard and tears slip quietly into Rosie's hair.

There's a brown envelope beside the blue and white salt cellar on the kitchen shelf. It arrived through the post a few days ago, not long after the trip to the library. Kezia eyes it when she hands Grandma a wad of toilet roll. She's not been able to read it, for Grandma hasn't left her in the kitchen alone. On the morning the postman stuck it through the letterbox, Grandma sent Kezia and Rosie upstairs to play, even though they were supposed to tidy away their colouring books and crayons. As they walked upstairs, Kezia hung back and, through the banisters, saw Grandma and Grandad huddle round the letter at the kitchen table. She thinks it's from Roy's son.

She's burning to read it. She steals another glance at the envelope and lets Grandma hug her for a while, so she can crane her neck and squint at the typed address. The summer has been a mosaic of hints and overheard remarks. They gather around Kezia like stepping stones. She thinks of Sherlock Holmes and the way he gathers clues. And then she thinks of Grandad's pipe and can't help giggle.

Grandma feels her shiver and releases her. 'What are you laughing at, sweetheart?'

'I was thinking of the time Grandad put snuff in his pipe instead of tobacco.' It had happened at the start of the summer, when watching Grandad smoke his pipe was still a novelty. Rosie and Kezia would hang back after tea, fascinated at the puff-puff of smoke. 'His face went purple!'

Rosie is sniggering, too. A bright moment, and Grandma can't help but smile. Her face cracks open and she seems relieved. 'Your Grandad will always be a turnip.'

That makes the girls laugh even more, thrilled that Grandma has said something actually funny. As they slink outside to the garden, Rosie mutters 'turnip, turnip, turnip-head' under her breath.

They are sitting on the path just outside the back door when the car pulls up. Kezia looks up and sees it first – an orange Cortina, with brown panels on the bottom. Her stomach cramps immediately. She can only see part of the car through the garden gate but knows the door handles will be rusty and there'll be a torn sticker saying Sheffield Wednesday on the rear passenger window. It's Dad's car.

Rosie hasn't noticed. She's engrossed in another fairy picnic, for the azalea bush has flowered unexpectedly and she's got a handful of purple petals. It's a sign of how sure she is that Grandma will let her get away with anything at the moment, for she wouldn't have pulled apart so pretty a flower at the start of the summer. She's humming as she sets the petals on a green leaf. Then, realising Kezia isn't playing, looks up.

'Kez?' Finally she sees him.

A thin man stands at the gate. He's wearing a white shirt and blue jeans, a collection of pens in his top pocket. He's got plastic sunglasses on, but the girls know his face. His hair is longer than they remember. He's wearing the same trainers he always wore when he wasn't at work.

Rosie's squeal is sharp and piercing. She's on her feet. But she doesn't run towards him. Instead she shrieks again, loud enough for Kezia to clap her hands over her ears. Blood pounds at Kezia's temples, like the sea, and she blinks over and over. She can't understand Rosie's reaction, only that it's savage and could sear birds from the trees. She looks at the gate and at the man, and then back at the gate. Suddenly she feels sorrowful that Grandad hasn't got round to repainting it. The wood is colour sky-blue and leaves flakes on your hands when you touch it.

The shed and back doors are flung open simultaneously, and Grandma and Grandad appear. Both are wide-eyed and terrified, and Kezia can see they are sure they are about to discover that one of the girls has hurt themselves, badly.

Why else that awful noise? Then Grandma and Grandad see the man at the garden gate. Grandma puts a hand to her chest and slumps against the wall. Grandad rocks on his heels.

It's Dad. He's smiling. He removes his glasses and Kezia see he's grown a moustache. It quite suits him and, amidst her shock, she thinks again how handsome he is. His teeth glitter brilliantly in the morning sun.

'Hello,' he says, and steps through the gate. The latch makes a tiny metallic click like knives shuffling over each other in the cutlery drawer. It's enough of a sound to make Grandma and Grandad move.

'Girls, inside please,' Grandma says. She steps away from the wall and marches in front of Kezia and Rosie. She puts her hands on her hips, as if she's making herself as large as possible. Shoulders back, neck up. 'Kezia, take your sister into the kitchen.'

'Edith, there's no need for that,' Dad says. He's still smiling and his voice is calm. The sunglasses dangle carelessly in his fingers and Kezia is hit by a memory – Dad was holding a letter at the top of the stairs, the day Rosie fell. Thin blue paper, the faintest image of an aeroplane in the corner. Dad had been angry. Kezia creeps closer to Grandma.

'You need to leave.' Grandad's found his voice but it's scratchy, as if he's swallowed nails.

'I only want to see my children,' Dad says. His grin widens. 'You've both caught the sun! Rosie, you look like a little nut!'

Rosie mumbles something and joins Kezia, clamping herself to Grandma's side. Kezia can feel Grandma's legs shiver and wildly thinks of raspberry ripple ice-cream, and the swirl of berry jam through vanilla. Kezia's hand curls out and she catches Rosie's fingers.

'Visitation is to be arranged through your solicitor,' Grandad says. 'I've told you that before, Philip.'

'No need to be formal.'

'It's for their safety.' Grandad takes a step towards him. The back of his shirt has come loose and hangs over his corduroy trousers. Kezia sees the edge of the string he ties the trousers up with and her heart leaks, oozing towards Grandad. She realises, for the first time, that he is shorter than Dad. He's sunburnt on the top of his bald head and it shines with vulnerability.

'You're being ridiculous,' Dad says. He doesn't move but his body seems to shift, shoulders flexing. 'I'm no danger to my children. Girls, haven't you missed me?'

Kezia starts to cry. She blinks fiercely, trying to hold tears back, but they spill down her face anyway. She doesn't have any toilet roll to wipe them away so presses her face into Grandma's side, breathing in the smell of dinner. Another rabbit stew is on the stove. Rosie squeezes Kezia's hand.

'Let's go inside,' Grandma says. 'Philip, you should leave. If you don't disappear within five minutes, I'm calling the police.'

'And say what, Edith?' Dad moves now, and walks down

the path towards them. 'That you're preventing a father from seeing his children? Go head, ring them. I'll be pleased to tell them about their mother, abandoning them for her fancy man.'

'Anna hasn't abandoned them,' Grandad says.

Dad laughs. Kezia hates the sound. It's a swallowed, round sound, as if Dad has rocks in his mouth. She remembers it from before, from before the time Rosie fell down the stairs. 'She's coming back tomorrow!' she bursts, and then claps her hand over her mouth.

'Then I'm just in time, aren't I? I wonder what the police would make of her plan to take you away.'

'That's enough,' Grandad says. He rolls his sleeves up. His navy tattoos look like bruises, faded and blue, but he stands with his hands on his hips and they shimmer in the midday heat. 'Just get back in your car and leave, Phil.'

'No, I don't think I will. I want to see my girls. That's not too much to ask, is it? They should know what's going on. You know, being taken away to Germany to live on an army base.'

Then Rosie does burst into tears. She buries her face in Grandma's waist, pressing her mouth against Grandma's side so that only her hair can be seen. Grandma makes an exasperated sound.

'Go away,' she hisses. 'You're frightening them.'

Dad hooks his thumbs into his back pockets and Kezia wonders if he's doing so in order to hold himself back. She feels very afraid now, and longs for Grandad to step away.

She thinks of small arms and legs, rolling down carpeted stairs, an ocean of tumbling. And then she thinks of the hound and brave Sherlock Holmes, stalking the moors, even when the moon was sallow and the colour of old egg. Sherlock is brave. She remembers what Miss Sybil said, that day at the library. *Be brave.*

She takes a deep breath and releases Rosie's hand, and steps away from Grandma, further down the path towards Dad. Grandma gasps and reaches out, fingers scuffing the top of Kezia's shoulder. But Kezia doesn't stop and moves closer, until she's right in front of the man who stepped out of the gold car.

'Kezia,' Grandad says.

Dad's smile widens and he extends his arms. 'Sweetheart,' he says.

Kezia shakes her head. Words crowd in her mouth, and she doesn't know what she's going to say until she says it. 'Do you know what a bread poultice is, Dad?'

'A what?'

'A poultice. Grandad taught me about them. It's hot water and bread. You mash it up so it's like Plasticine. We've had to put them on Rosie's arm because it still hurts her.'

Dad's expression doesn't change. Kezia can see all his teeth. She blinks hard and carries on.

'This summer we've caught Jack's ferrets that escaped into the garden, and made fairy picnics from Grandma's roses. We've had fish and chips and when Andrew married Fergie, we had cherry pop.' Kezia starts to count out things on her fingers. 'We know how to find tomatoes that are just the right kind of red and Grandad swings us on the allotment gate. I made a gypsy caravan from a cardboard tube but I left it out in the rain, and I'm still sad about that.'

'Well, Kezia...' Dad starts to say.

'No, that's not everything. Don't you want to know what we've done?' Kezia hears Grandma begin to hum and knows she doesn't have much time. 'Grandma made me a rainbow jumper for my birthday and I now love Sherlock Holmes. He was a brave man. He solved mysteries. And we spoke to Uncle Andy in Australia. He's getting married to a lady called Melinda and we sent her a bracelet. Rosie chose it. She's got an eye for it, apparently.'

Grandad laughed softly.

'And Andy said something else, Dad,' Kezia says.

'What's that, Kezia?' Dad asks faintly. He's tilted his head to the side and is glaring at her.

Kezia licks her dry lips. Her belly and bum puckers a little. She knows she will get into the most awful trouble for what she's about to say, but the words are already on her tongue. She has to, she has to, just as she has to stand on the allotment gate for all of the swings, and has to eat rabbit stew again, and has to reach for Grandma's arm when a sad story comes on the news and laugh at one of Grandad's tall tales.

'He said – he said you'd fucked up. And he's right. You've fucked up. In fact, you're a fuck-up.'

Rosie squeals and Kezia hears Grandma clap her hand to

her mouth. She's twitching inside and prays she won't wet her pants, for her stomach now feels so loose she thinks it might come sieving down her legs. Grandad is choking, and then suddenly throwing his head back and braying into the blue sky.

Only Dad has the reaction Kezia expects adults would have at the words. She's a little girl, after all, and *language like that is appalling on a child*. She's heard Mrs Hartley say as much to Grandma when they've stopped for a chat – the boys who hang around the Bottle Shop of an evening are an *absolute* menace and the *gutter* mouths! Dad is glinting at her, eyes as black as raisins.

'Delightful,' he says. 'Is that what you've learned this summer? I should smack your bottom.'

'No, you should leave.' Grandad says. He's moved to stand next to Kezia and his sandpaper hand is on her shoulder. She loves the weight of it, gnarled old fingers pressing down, a line of safety. 'Make arrangements to see your children through your solicitor. This isn't over, not by a long way."

Kezia can see there isn't really much else to say. A small part of her feels sorry for Dad – the part that cares about burgers at the football game but doesn't think about the time he was mad at her when she was travel sick in his car. The tucked away memory of him teaching her to play draughts, frowning at her in combat. But, more than anything, she wants him to leave.

Then Dad shrugs. An exaggerated, don't-care motion

and, lopsided smile in Rosie's direction, turns and walks back through the gate. He clicks it shut and stands the other side of it. Kezia holds her breath.

'I'll be in touch,' he says. And then he gets in his car and drives away.

They stand silently on the path for a while. Heat beats down on their heads.

'I don't want to hear that kind of language come out of your mouth again, my dear,' Grandma says eventually. She smooths down her tabard and her face is pink. 'I never heard the like.'

'Oh, you have, Edith,' Grandad chuckles. He fights to control his face, flesh rising and falling, a frown and a grin. Then he gives up and simply beams. 'You're married to a sailor, after all.'

Grandma huffs and tugs Rosie back down the path towards the house. 'I expect we'll get a call from his solicitor soon enough.'

'It's going to be interesting tomorrow,' Grandad says. He doesn't look in the least bit bothered. 'Good job we've got Roy's son coming, eh?'

The path feels unsteady under Kezia's feet and she tastes the world of adults, mixing everything up, frightening her. She can't bear to pick apart what it means for Roy's son, coming to the house tomorrow. When Mum would be there, presumably. It's too big and scary an idea and she senses it has knives and spikes to it.

For now, it's enough to slip underneath Grandma's arm

and wedge into the warm space of her armpit, and elbow Rosie gently to tell her she loves her. And for Grandad to giggle to himself and head over to the allotment to fetch raspberries for tea.

Acknowledgements

Thank you, Claire, for allowing me to plunder your memories – you were always much better than me at remembering places and things.

I have been fortunate to know and love strong women who played a vital role in my childhood, or provided a bedrock of friendship as I grew as a writer. Aunties Cilla and Fran, and Ange (Kiwi Ma) – to all with love.

About the Author

Rebecca Burns is an award-winning writer of short stories. Her story collections, *Catching the Barramundi* (2012) and *The Settling Earth* (2014) were both longlisted for the Edge Hill Short Story Award. She was nominated for a Pushcart Prize in 2011 and 2020, winner of the Fowey Festival of Words and Music Short Story Competition in 2013 (and runner-up in 2014), winner of the Black Pear Press Short Story Competition in 2014 and, in 2016, was listed for competitions including the Evesham Festival of Words and Music, the Chipping Norton Festival, the Sunderland Short Story Award, and the Green Lady Press Short Story Award. She has also been profiled as part of the University of Leicester's Grassroutes Project that showcases the 50 best transcultural writers in the county.

Her debut novel, *The Bishop's Girl*, was published by Odyssey Books in September 2016, followed by a third short story collection, *Artefacts and Other Stories* (2017), a sequel novel to *The Settling Earth*, called *Beyond the Bay*, was published in 2018. Her first novella, *Quilaq*, was published by Next Chapter in 2020.

Her website is at www.rebecca-burns.co.uk, and you can follow her on Twitter at @Bekki66 and on Facebook at Rebecca Burns.